After the Water Receded

After the Water Receded

DAVID T. BRADFORD

RESOURCE *Publications* · Eugene, Oregon

AFTER THE WATER RECEDED

Resource Publications
An Imprint of Wipf and Stock Publishers
199 W. 8th Ave., Suite 3
Eugene, OR 97401

www.wipfandstock.com

PAPERBACK ISBN: 979-8-3852-2525-5
HARDCOVER ISBN: 979-8-3852-2526-2
EBOOK ISBN: 979-8-3852-2527-9

Squat down. See what I've held so long in this hand, tightly clenched, the fist jammed in my pocket since leaving. You remember. The fingers uncurl painfully. There isn't the usual feeling. A rosy aura recedes from the fingernails as blood flushes the white crescent of each quick. Blisters! I've been burned without knowing. Now, in my palm, see the stone, its milky glare faceted in a thousand watery surfaces. Please, take it! I've brought this for you.

Contents

Contents

Preface

THE PIECES THAT FORM this collection were written over several decades. In general, the shorter the piece, the earlier its date of composition. The vignettes and prose poems in Chapters 1, 2, and 4 were written in the 1970s and 1980s. The lengthier pieces about the artists Klee, Mondrian, and Duchamp in Chapter 8 were written two or more decades later. The pieces completed most recently—"The Big Ship," "Eye of the Circle," and "Chandler, Hammett, and the Harrowing of Hell"—underwent their final revision in 2025. Years passed before I felt sufficient detachment to edit and revise much of this work. Premature efforts at revision were instant benumbing failures.

A range of literary forms is represented in these pages: stories, dream reports, historical fiction, epistolary exchanges, lyrical vignettes. "The Celestial Jester" and "The Crooked Man and the Maids of Salt" are tales. "Art in Due Season" is an autobiographical essay about artistic creativity—it could pass as memoir. "Reported by a Respected Ethnographer" is a parody of scholarly publications. The longer, richer "Eye of the Circle" grades from parody into character analysis and the description of an extraordinary form of spatial perception. Its central figure is Edmond Teste, the strange character created by the poet Paul Valéry. I reimagine Teste, examine his talents and cultural setting, and investigate an experimental log written by Valéry under Teste's name.

The individual chapters tend to form coherent wholes based on similarities of form or content. For example, Chapter 1 is composed of short pieces on deathbed scenes and fatal disability. Many pieces in Chapter 4 describe extraordinary deviations from the normal experience of self-embodiment, some of which are ecstatic. Chapter 7 focuses on personal artwork, real and imagined. Chapter 8 includes three works of historical fiction, two of which take the form of a soliloquy by a famous modern artist dated to the indicated calendar year.

The concluding chapter contains two stories: "Ominous Signals, Deathly Quiet" and "Waves of the Glorious Splendor (Isaac of Nineveh, 7th c.)." The first is the report of a journey through apocalyptic circumstances written in the style I call visionary prose. The second story, another historically based soliloquy, is devoted to Isaac of Nineveh, a revered seventh-century Eastern Christian ascetic. The two stories are paired opposites, like a disease and its cure. The opening sentence of "Ominous Signals, Deathly Quiet" is the source of the collection's title: "I will speak without codes or sleight of hand and tell what I saw after the water receded." Visionary prose informs other stories. Obvious examples are "The Perfect Consumer" and "Chandler, Hammett, and the Harrowing of Hell."

This collection coheres around four prominent themes: death and the scenes that surround it; spiritual intent and mystical experience; the nature of creativity and the production of artwork; and the tests and challenges of inhabiting a physical body. A fifth, sparsely represented theme might be called Our Dystopian Future.

1. Fearful of Death

The Convalescent Home

A three-cornered courtyard surfaced with tile, outlined with shrubbery. To the far side, a sparse grove of sapling oak woven with brassy light and a pair of silver rails. I sit in the armchair, he sits on the bed, glazed eyes framed by a skewed corona of white hair. The transistor radio plays a tinny divertissement to which he keeps time with the tapping exploration of his leathery tongue. The tune concludes with the train's passing, clapping steel setting Friday's rhythms against the continuo of the whistle's full wail. Now I stand in the flood tide washing away the brown powder walls of our small room.

Fearful of Death

Fearful of death she spoke succinctly, prolonged reflection permitting the formulation of her most profound worry: "My space will be left vacant." But the same thought is a comfort when applied to an empty seat at a reserved performance. Assured of having space, one rests easily until time to occupy it. She would be at peace while living if she transformed the space she worries over leaving by letting it billow from the margin of her body and dissolve in the blue-rimmed bowl of the horizon. The space she worries over leaving, now as thick and heavy as her body, would then engulf the arena centered around the seat she desperately hopes to reserve.

Unwillingness to Approach the Deathbed

What demands are made by a husband of fifty years whose mind has vanished, whose stale voice beckons from a small odorous cavern? Fidgeting in the hallway when invited to enter, she said, "No, he won't recognize me." Her fear can be put into words: If I am not recognized as myself—if I am nothing more than a touch on his palm, fingertip pressure on his eyelid, words whispered in his ear, then I have already vanished. Am I nothing more than threaded moments, beads of sensation tumbling into disarray? Powerful threats, no doubt: first, to her mask, and second to her sense of self. The first indicates loss of face, the second risks the sacrifice of her mind. She is not alone in such fear. Smugness is a fool's dance. Would you swim nude, knowing sharks were seen close to shore? Would you watch yourself dissolve, knowing your disappearance will coincide with the moment of self-observation?

Consider her suggestion that his oxygen be cut. She presupposes an ineradicable point of reference—a self that transcends the body, and from the depths of humane feeling rises her desire to alleviate its suffering that it might pass to the realm where she, too, will live forever in a world of unchanging gestures. Blessed be human affections.

Died Last Night

(1) The lady died last night. Leukemia, blood pale as her cumulus heaps of white hair. Implacable ardor perfectly contained, calm as a napping baby. Now she is exploded into the aether. Her courage endured her body's recoiling from the spirit's final leap for freedom. Those at the bedside took no comfort in her release. Their eyes were sliced through with the razor edge of pain. Their eyes were moons perspiring crystals with liquid centers.

(2) An old hunter who trafficked in ivory along the Angolan coast told of seeing a herd of elephants exit the forest a quarter mile from the very blue sea before sidling into surging waves—great billows banking against the flanks of cows, their closely watched calves and the ancient bulls, heads bobbing with the weight of ivory. A single lion roars on the white sand beach, molten light spilling from its flared mane.

2. Rumors Firsthand

Half Idiot, Half Drunk

Along the sidewalk he came, pausing with each stroke of his cane, one foot stepping lightly, the other shuffling and tamping the ground before absorbing the weight of his body. During one pause he drooled and spit, during another he addressed the air with disgruntled animation. He spoke to persons unseen—or, if not unseen, he must have spoken to me. I was nearby. I can make substantial the air he has charged with his imagination. I must know this man with crazy eyes, a grizzled face and gnarled fingers, his khakis cinched tightly around his thighs. I will know this man, and do so instantly, and whether he experiences our secret acquaintance amounts to nothing. Dare I know him, and do so instantly, binding profound indifference and an irrevocable need to touch misery external to myself? I know the means of our commingling. Its preliminaries are visual. I must look and see. I must apprehend his bearing, his physiognomy, through its external form. Once itching from his beard and sensing the drafts passing across his sunburnt chest, once reeling from intoxication and stung with the needles of paralysis, I would seize his glance and know those with whom he spoke. I would hear their voices and feel the galvanizing effect of their conversation, meanwhile the pedestrians passing nearby would become spectral shapes, pale and washed of life. I would know his misery and sense a world populated with the figures of madness.

What would I become upon exchanging my own self for his? What remains after trading another body for one's own? What remains is a spark of attention brutally refined, radiant and discerning, its center missing. What remains is profound indifference paired with an irrevocable need to touch misery external to oneself. What can be said about this spark of attention that aims each day to become fire? Would I flash or would that man? Who is consumed by the tiny conflagration that signals the event of selfless intimacy?

Blushing Pink Gentleness

Airplanes continue to buzz the house. Those approaching the nearby airport rumble and gasp while passing over the roof. Picture frames rattle, glassware vibrates in the kitchen cabinet. Air traffic had yet to erect its gutters of sound yesterday morning when I walked to the garden in the half-light of dawn. Vapor blanketed the yard, diffusing and softening angled beams of light. The tight-fisted bloom of a gnarled rose was tinctured air glowing violet. Then began the roar, a descending plane close enough to cast a nearby shadow. What could I do but welcome the challenge and whisper a stubborn greeting? So began the subtle project of matching the flower and the roar, combining sound, form, and color. Imagine a bloom of thunder—a blushing pink gentleness whose pulsing chord shook the ground on which I stood.

Blind Man Standing

A blind man stands at the busy corner, his upright bearing modeling a military physique. Dignity, vigilance, the aplomb of perfect quiet—all meshing before my eyes. Pedestrians pass by and around. A speeding car grazes his cane—the pinprick sensation quivers like a violin string. For him the ambient noise is an invisible net cinched tightly around his body, a discernible pattern of astutely gauged sounds. On rare occasions, suddenly and effortlessly, he becomes a transparent globe of palpable awareness, the center of a perfect sphere of sound. Sounds rebound from concave surfaces, and trees gather strength from invisible roots. So, with him. His body is a pillar wide and tall. The earth's surface is neither a barrier nor a support, and the sky no longer poses a limit. Where, at these moments, does he stand? The position of others is relative to his. Beneath him, dense silence falling toward the earth's center; above, the orchestrated sounds of a city roofed with light.

A Seed So Small

An infinitesimal seed settles on the silver blade of a vacuum-encased scalpel. Its rocking descent is patterned like a boat traversing velvety waves in nighttime darkness. It touches and rebounds, then touches again before it comes to rest and begins absorbing the antiseptic air within the glass container. Now, under pressures of life, the seed sprouts tendrils that curl like grapevines winding through latticed slats. Days pass in which inhuman increments of time mark the genesis and swelling of translucent cells, the coupling and dispersion of atoms, the inaudible grating of molecules of steel. Mark your vocabulary! Erase the word *inanimate*.

A Single Hook is Chosen

Ordinarily a single hook is chosen, one with multiple barbs designed to anchor the shaft deeply in the gill. Once baited and the line weighted, the hook is dropped toward the bottom. Once set, it is jerked to shore, where the torsion and silvery turning come to rest, the fish sated to death with oxygen. But there is an alternative to this violent procedure. Release a dozen hooks, unbated, and beside them suspend another dozen, also unbated. Tantalize the fish, draw and shape its fascination. When it turns to one hook, distract it with another, then a third and fourth, until finally the creature is a bundle of luminous flashes, a burst of snapshots, each of its scales known from a dozen angles. This is the secret, true to thought: familiarity is the enemy. Seek to know your mind off-guard, watch for its spark of recognition.

Certain Stars

Scientists say certain stars are so distant that they have long since been extinguished when we first see their light. The same point, made differently, recalls a constellation warmer than starlight and more habitable than one explored with telescopes. My grandmother, turning from the crib, says aloud, "Imagine! I've outlived a star." Thirty years later, that baby, now grown, says, "Think of it! A star's death attended my birth." And only yesterday, upon entering the nursery and seeing moonlight spread across her face, I whispered, "Her smile brightens something dense and dark in outer space."

Mango and Orange, Plum and Peach

Each morning, he fetches pounds of chipped ice from a downtown warehouse before pushing his cart to the busy corner where he stands throughout the day—a beacon of quiet amid passing cars, a mute spokesman for simplicity. Aside from exchanging customers' money for paper cones filled with sweetened color, his only activity is to discard melted cones and substitute fresh ones in the notched board resting on the cart lid. Bright cool satisfaction tinted with pristine specimens of the rainbow. Is his appeal the sale of color combined with cold, or does he draw and hold my attention because of the simplicity of his service? Neither. His appeal is my fantasy of the routine life mimicked in his neutral expression. Serving only gravity and heat, he is the coincidence of a bright sun and empty sky during a momentary pause of commerce.

> *Ice! Ice!*
> *Red and green,*
> > *strawberry and grape.*
> *Mango and orange,*
> > *plum and peach.*
> *Ice! Ice!*

Eleusis

I used to play flute in the cave at Eleusis before quitting that miserable job. It was dark and cold, and there was nothing to see except mindless Athenians led in circles by bald priests. There were rats at the crossing and when I stepped into the boat they raced to bite my feet. For a little extra I promised not to tell it is only a man playing flute when the torches are lit and a slave girl hardly out of her father's house who beats tambourine. They knew more about her than I first thought. The stain shows when you squeeze that many pomegranates to sweeten that much flesh.[1]

Big Tex

The clash and odors of the midway yield to the stately promenade of bored freaks. A man shaped like a seal levers open a sagging newspaper while lounging lengthwise on a sweat-soaked bench. He aims an icy glare at the squinting crowd and mutters beneath his breath: "What a fate—thalidomide made me the butt of fascination and hate!" An exhibit featuring prison life is meant to reform juvenile delinquents. The barker's shifty gaze targets uniforms and stripes. A pasty woman survives a dozen blades that pierce her wooden box. The visible part of her body is an emerald tubular snake. Teenage girls peck and chatter while circling a strongman standing upright on his barrel perch. They reach and touch his barbell before the entire covey scatters. Garish tin monsters tremble above the ticket booth for *Ride à La Lune*—a clattering machine designed for a cartoon moon-shot flight. Krishna's devotees circulate in turmeric chadors, distributing pamphlets at Big Tex's feet. Their happy chanting survives the boombox twang of a papier-mâché cowboy so huge he straddles the churning crowds passing through clicking turnstiles and open gates.

The Exiled Jews

The Jews purged from Córdoba are assigned boats moored in Lisbon—boats of balsam strapped with bloody sinew. Pale-complected men, bearded and bespectacled. Raven-haired women nursing babies bound in velvet. A fleet of snow set for deep-water harbors of clotted ash. Blown landward, they toss silver coins to circling sharks. Jeering boys pelt their boats from the Normandy coast. Starving off the coast of France, they soon debark in Flanders. The snap and crack of clogs on cobblestone veil softly shuffling feet. They become merchants and build two synagogues, the second so beautiful the sailors are awed: "See what has become of the Jews of Córdoba!"

Breathless

1. If one's breath were lost, where would it go?
   - a. over the horizon
   - b. down a well
   - c. into a burrow at the base of a tree
2. If all our breaths were lost, where would they go?
   - a. to the moon
   - b. toward the sun
   - c. down a ravine at the bottom of the ocean
3. Once breathless, what have we left?
   - a. starlight and the locution of planets
   - b. the Mariana Trench gone dry and filled with roses

The Cafeteria

Rice cakes sweetened with honey are distributed at double doors broad as the portal of Hades. Ease forward, first in line. Gesture toward a hamburger patty, the puddle of relaxed green beans, the cherry pie with a waxy glaze, and await their insertion beneath the fogged glass by a plump hand displaying pink fingernail polish. Tray in hand, be seated, observe your neighbors. Faces bent over plates for eternity. Eyes shadowed with tedium unrelieved by sleep. Minds surfacing from cups of coffee like lolling fish. Conversations repeated time and again for all time. Years pass before the adults exhaust their store of memories. Children remain seated and never grow. But I am the voyeur—surging visceral acid allows me to eat and run, fetching a mint from the cashier and tossing it unwrapped to the dog howling outside the doors broad as the portal of Hades.

A Single Player Holds Cards

A single player holds cards, the rest have folded. He squints and nods, signaling readiness to play. The dealer steadies her green eyeshade, then snaps her head side to side, swiveling cottony braids of white hair. The paired holes above her cleft lip swell with each breath. He tosses three jacks. Her lips part momentarily, her tongue in full view—pink like a Murex and ridged with spines. She turns four queens in slow succession.

Houston

(1) Recall the serial killer who liked teenage boys, a half-dozen buried beneath his grandparents' lakeside cottage, others within cypress groves lining the Gulf Coast of Texas. Insouciance muted the visionary display of terror and grimaces when his eyes traced the headlights of a swaying Plymouth traveling macadam highways softening in the heat of summer. His mind—corroded with fumes spewed from flares and factories rendering gas from black crude. His trunk heaped with body parts, a rake, and two shovels. Houston: a thousand scarlet sunsets gloating over mirrored office buildings. Houston: a bloody anus airborne and blinking.

(2) Should I mention the message etched by bare branches on the window of a yellow school bus, or the boy with auburn hair who struggled to decipher its script? I saw a tree tell a boy in a difficult language of a breeze that cloaks trees in leaves and strips them in autumn and scratches glass to warn boys who disembark from yellow school buses.

(3) "I will bathe them in vodka and soften their skin with blood-saturated gauze before our medical procedure of sex in the raw. Life is a flicker anticipating an explosion. It is not gusto I favor but the knife and the explosion."

Infernal

An enormous machine approaches, running opposite the direction of my bike. Between us, the freshly painted stripe on new asphalt. It lumbers forward, a tumbling giant, scoop inverted tongue-to-cheek. Invoking calm and breathing deeply, I see the machine approach in silence, its bouncy rhythm mimicking the stuttering advance of silent movies. I see slices of time strung front to back, the machine rising and settling, the husky driver rocked side to side, gripping the wheel. I attend, as if counting beads on a string, and so appease the furor of the machine until the moment of this word's arrival: *infernal.*

Larvae

They must have been maggots of the common fly—cylindrical deposits, squat and bulging at the center, pumped from tiny sphincters of gelatin cavities. Opalescent pearls, the fruit of buzzing annoyance. Their spasmodic leaps resemble a worm tossed to writhe on heated tin. Lacking scales and yet reptilian, each disjointed segment contributes tiny seizures to the chorea of an electrocuted centipede. The blunt end of their bodies forms a circular concavity ringed with pale, delicate tubers, like the encrusted face of a mole or the beak of a gesturing anemone. Each has the whitish color of coagulated grease and is sufficiently translucent to disclose a thin black filament at its tip—a live wire, the source of the mouthless appetite driving its parasitic motility. These semblances of a creature dropped from a bird crushed in the street.

Vaudeville Stage

A vaudeville stage lit and glowing, beeswax candles shedding tallowy light. The clown enters; murmuring ceases. He rips his threadbare tunic and stutters incoherently before he grips his neck and pretends strangulation. A minute more, the crowd erupts in jeers and the curtains lurch in a blur of green velvet. The master of ceremonies enters—prancing, chortling, pumping his stovepipe hat. Backstage, the clown's tears coagulate like glassy rubies.

3. Stories

A Bird Called Repeatedly

A bird called repeatedly during the counseling session, its tweedling the counterpoint to the rasping drone of cicadas. Shadowy wings flickered across the opposite wall before the bird lit in a tree visible from her seat but not from mine. She was entranced by the sound, deeply so, to the point of suddenly changing forms. No longer human, she had sprouted wings, densely feathered and held in taut suspension. Her cheeks were scarlet, her grotesque beak curved and nicked. Her eyes were perfectly round, same as the irises, which filled the white sclera with blue the color of sapphire. Her eyelids had vanished and her forehead had narrowed to a simian slant. Fire billowed along the edge of her scalp—flames blown backward, swirling over her skull, sucking drafts of air and creating a huffing sound like wind passing through a grove of trees. I did not see a single bead of perspiration or the faintest blister, and yet her face was surrounded with a corona of fire. We sat in silence. I was entranced.

A nurse walked the hospital corridor, keys jangling. The seclusion room door clicked shut, its muffled rattle heightening the tedium of the summer afternoon. The atmosphere within the room was thick like impenetrable cloud cover. Her beak, I decided, had been nicked from husking nuts and seeds. I checked my watch. After what seemed an interminable amount of time, she raised her arms and drew her hands through the fire before lowering them directly in front of my face. Resting on her palms was a faceted stone clear as lead crystal. The room darkened at that moment, or else the stone's brightness dulled the room's light by comparison. I studied the stone and, upon noticing its many facets, a web of cracks shot through its center. The stone crumbled, its residue no more than a tiny heap of ash. I raised my eyes at this point and saw that her true appearance had been restored. She looked normal, altogether so. We talked a few more minutes before I ended the session. Neither of us mentioned the stone, her beak, or the fire. She said nothing suggesting awareness of her transformation, and I did not betray my fear upon seeing her flesh burning.

She was an interesting person, highly attractive, her problems little different than those of other young women of her age, station, and beauty—the chief difference being her lightning quickness in shifting between fatuous social patter and exceedingly intense emotion. Her hospitalization was more happenstance than justification for psychiatric treatment. The doctors, puzzled over her diagnosis, settled on a generic term that implied equivocation. I had difficulty thinking of her in clinical terms and have grown less adept in such matters since dissatisfaction with my work led to a complete change of career.

My Friend Travels First Class

The forces that arranged our first meeting were highly unusual. He later said he had been "harassed by the Devil" and subjected to "literal Hell." Thinking to confront the Evil One, he addressed the darkness late one evening: "If you intend to carry on like this, why not take the form of a tall, dark intellectual type?"

His plan was to arrange a battle. Were the Devil to adopt a single form rather than dissemble and manifest its purpose in a melee of temptations and attacks, my friend would have it out once for all with the Enemy. Two days later, he met me: a tall, dark, intellectual type. I was a real person who fit his fantasy of a satanic Faust. I remember his persistent examination of my interest in mysticism. His carefully composed manner of poorly informed curiosity was a weak disguise for the intensity of his interest. I had abandoned art by this time, directing my fascination with the ineffable toward just this area of study. His curiosity had a basis in fact.

Soon after our first meeting, he dreamed once again of fighting the Devil: "I was seated in a chair in the middle of an empty room. The Devil—a scaly, foul-looking creature—attacked me. We battled. I threw him down the stairs and won an overwhelming victory. It was the most action-packed dream I've ever had. Normally I dream in slow motion."

Of special interest is his oneiric means of anticipating our meeting—his searching demonic lens, which targeted a person recently baptized in fire and spirit. I think one of us was already falling, or was fearful of doing so, and in retrospect I find it hard to know which of us had Lucifer as a brother. Certainly not my friend, judging from his black suit and white collar and his punctual attendance at Mass. I was the one who skirted the edge of disobedience rather than tow the barge of pious submission. I was the one who cultivated a reverent agnosticism to cool the intensity of touches of fire.

I once told him: "I try to make use of everything." To which he replied: "I know, but there are some things I won't touch, won't even come near."

I asked if he had found traces of the demonic in my character. He said, "not at all," then continued: "But if I had, I wouldn't have come near you. I wouldn't have touched you with a ten-foot pole." Momentarily his expression softened, and it may have been a genuinely gracious impulse that prompted his saying: "Yes, I would have!"

My friend travels first class, hires porters to carry his luggage. I travel lightly and change cars frequently. We meet still, our affection grows. Men make better friends than angels or demons.

The Crooked Man and the Maids of Salt

I saw a hunchbacked man lift brightly colored piano notes from a wooden tub and set each to dry with clothespins he took from the muslin bag strapped around his neck, dangling to his thighs. A dozen notes hung from a line of hemp twine strung between two trees bent leeward by constant sea breeze. I saw a gallery of pliable primaries, a jazzy tune arched skyward, a rainbow twittering in salty air, a spidery canopy of windblown melody casting moth-like shadows on the bone-white shore. Braced against a tree, the crooked man sniffed its aromatic bark before inhaling a great draught of air, his chest swelling in exact proportion to his lumpy backside. For a moment, no more, his crooked spine straightened like a shot arrow. Drawing a mother-of-pearl panpipe from his bag and anchoring it tightly with a toothy bite, he snorted and whistled and craned his neck. He blew a reedy tune before returning the pipe to the bag and beginning the story I heard while hidden in a nearby grove:

> I lived the boyish wish to become a picador and drive the brutal pike into the great bull's saddle-back neck. My soul was a lamprey fixed to a ship of dreams. But what future awaits a stooped boy whose measly body struggles under the weight of a single feather? So I continued to dream of a gallivanting horse bearing my poised arm toward strong prey.
>
> My mother was an ogress, the mistress of our bridge. My play-mate brother was a slouch-shouldered troll. We fished in a creek passing between muddy banks in the northern forests. We caught crayfish in nets woven from our mother's hair. We scavenged in the nearby trash-heap badlands replenished daily by loud trucks. We made slingshots of willow saplings and peppered the dragon-flies swarming in summer's clicking air. We skewered and roasted sparrows over the evening fire and served minnows in pungent broth. We hooked, trapped, caught and cooked. Mighty hunters, masterful little beasts. The wood was ours.
>
> Our mother took pride in her boys and was happy with our lot until she heard of a spot farther on, past the western lake. She led us there—no questions asked, no answers proffered. We were

brave and walked with determination. "To the sea," she said, and so we went, all three, until grippe befell my brother and gout attacked his knees. He died, poor troll, and my mother and I passed alone. A motley pair, an ogress mother and her hunched child, we muffled our tears in nighttime's pillow. We walked in silence, desperate to find our way, until a dune-top vista revealed the blue horizon hemmed by a white sand shore.

My mother knew more than she had allowed. She taught the lay of the waves and the spiriferous coil of the shells we found washed ashore. My dreams were filled with seashells. The largest was home to a giant crab whose rugged mandibles pinched the rings of Saturn and the stellar threadwork upholding the silver platter of the moon.

I first heard the mermaids singing in the rustling of a passing storm. Blown landward on sea breeze, mixed with the tumult of knotted waves, their singing filled barren nights with the sweet balm of adventuresome longing. I fell under their sway, the lulling beauty of their songs. They took pleasure in my growing store of sea lore. They played pipes carved from mother-of-pearl. Their songs cast spells on the water—waves surging in gray eddies, crests intertwined and hovering delicately until their spindly dance collapsed into foaming pools. The maids of salt adopted me. I went willingly to sea, bidding goodbye to my ogress mother. Her farewell tears glistened in the distance, her black eyes shown at dusk. I followed the maids into the ocean depths but surfaced too often for their liking, until gills formed at the coccyx and my bubbling ceased to betray our invisible flights, our passage to deep havens of rest.

Each day brought new trials, and each trial brought a ravishing victory. Fleet of fin, flesh of fish, blood billowed when my rapier flashed. I guided mermaids enraptured with my beauty and protected their kin with sterling grace. When we cruised the sloughs and plumbed the deep, the most supple water creatures were left stranded, twisted in wrack and weed, bound in moss and kelp. I tamed waves rougher than scales on a crocodile tail. We sunned on black sand beaches under scudding clouds, beneath the golden clapper strung sky-high in the great turquoise bell. They set me upon a throne built of shells and gull wings. We feasted on lobster tails, the finest meat of the foaming deep. Supplicants gathered at my feet, scavengers followed in our wake. Those were days more royal than this sunny beach, more lovely than my children's salt-flecked feet.

Our days of glory ended violently when a fleet of whaling ships sailed amid my friends flaunting their green tails and white arms on ocean billows. The sailors let loose a harpoon salvo before launching the smaller boats. They surrounded and killed my maidenly friends. Salty tears mixed with saltier blood in the roiling acid of my grief. But honor spoke—my retreat became an outraged return. I was armed with angry vengeance. Finding those ships one night, I rammed my head against their hulls and punctured each one. Now was their turn to bubble in the bloody sputter of breath mixed with saltwater. I sported viciously among the sailors leaping free. Their death was a sweet token of exchange for the spent lives of my dear friends.

My sad heart weakened like a sickly gray mollusk and then it simply died. My grief-sunk desire was to drift downward to the ocean bottom, the rooftop sky's pillared base. Those who find dry land a happy place, who fear the haunted mood of the moth-wing deep, should turn their thoughts to my fair friends, their hearts to my flimsy house of tears.

The loneliness of months on the wide sea drove me landward. Swimming continuously, I finally saw a broad white hill of land. My sorry legs, vestiges of a former life, unfolded to the task of a bobbing weave to shore. I slept for days before awakening to a dozen children, dark as night, dancing round my driftwood hut. A dozen naked Negro children, their speckled rows of white teeth set within the most lovely of pristine smiles. Sons-to-be, and already I felt their love. One blew my pearly pipe, the single token of my days at sea.

"Give me my pipe!" I demanded, my croaking voice calling forth a ballyhoo of laughter. To which they shouted, "We love music!"

Then and there I conceded defeat and met their exclamation with willingness to follow. So we went, them laughing and dancing circles around my hobbling trot, the white beach a bright stage for our happy lot. Soon my back was swollen with painful blisters. They waited without murmuring when I asked for rest, then scurried ahead, darting between the water and the shore.

We turned inland and walked for hours until a sun-plaited cypress forest shown like a silhouette against the pink clouds of evening. This was their home and their mother's, a woman black and big as night, her smile a silver sliver. Her reach exceeded her girth, to this I attest. My back caused hardly a problem.

Since then, I have lived with the children and their mother. She launders their notes each morning in a sun-bleached wooden tub, and I set them to dry in the ocean breeze. Songs for the eye do satisfy the ear, but not without a sigh, for days past blow shoreward and the pearly pipe still brings tears to my eyes. I miss the giant crab, hermit of my mind, and hope that one day its curling shell will entwine its life with mine.

Days from Camp

Days from camp, their water gourds nearly empty, Bushman hunters walk the dry savannah of the Kalahari Desert. Giraffes stand idly in the distance, their necks craning toward the highest limbs of skeletal acacia. Their swishing tails count time in the clicking beat imposed by flying insects. Giraffe are called the Silent Ones, Children of the Moon, because they cannot growl or hoot or otherwise articulate communicative sounds.[2] They tip their ears, signal with blinks, and flutter their five-inch eyelashes.

The neck of one giraffe is pierced by a tiny Bushman arrow. The rest of the herd lopes away in rocking-horse fashion except for the wounded laggard whose trail of blood is tracked and followed by six pairs of feet. Braced against a tree, it emits wheezing sighs—the sliced wound quivers and vibrates like a reed when the winded animal breathes. Fright drives away all but the youngest hunter, who returns at dusk to care for the wounded animal. He patches the animal's neck with a poultice made of urine, saliva, and powdery red earth.

Days of hunger and thirst follow, and wondrous moonlit nights when the boy is cradled by four spindly legs and rocked to sleep in rising breeze. A jackal, the most shy of carnivores, approaches, its paws traversing the spidery prints of birds whose daytime perches are the horns of posing gazelle. Wild dogs pause and confer before slipping away. Hyenas sniff and pass, trailing jeers, stink, and laughter. Lions feign boredom, their leers fixed on blood. A gray wall of elephants forms across the morning horizon, blocking the sun.

The boy awakens suddenly. The giraffe, now standing bolt upright, tenses its neck and draws to the highest pitch a single note in which all the animals join—whistling, growling, stomping, blowing a chorus that shakes the blue vault of the sky and sets in motion crackling fissures running through the surrounding stones. Look now, the boy has vanished.

The Big Ship

On a dim afternoon this past winter, I departed the barbershop on Main Street and walked the half-block to the consignment store. Scanning for new arrivals, I discovered a set of six hand-painted plates of strange beauty. The plates were made in Japan, in the 1930s, by the company Meito China. Each one portrays a lake, an inland sea, and, to one side, a forested island, all in muted, richly saturated colors. Except for the thin gilt edge that encircles the rim, the painted scene is straight from Nature—no humans or manufactured dwellings. How lovely, I thought, reminded of the flowery plumage of silk kimonos.

Now, months later, I am distributing the plates to dear friends. You are among them. In studying your plate, you will see the shallows of a faraway shore, the Far Shore, where the Big Ship beaches after navigating the Major Divide under the pearly vapor of an iris-blue sky. I heard goats bleating when I waded ashore. I saw squirrels with teeth bright as chrome husking Brazil nuts the size of peaches. The beach was shiny and black, each grain of sand a perfect sphere. The waves rolled and curled and collapsed in time with the aimless tinkling of barely audible piano music. The sun was oval in shape, reminiscent of farm eggs, and the few clouds called to mind the blinking face of an owl. Striped ants raced at top speed, using their bodies to mark letters on the sand at my feel—*Welcome, mate!* had been written in a quivering cursive script.

I grew anxious and decided I must return home right away. I was greatly worried to see the Big Ship had already departed. Docked in a corner of its wide berth was a hand-hewn wooden canoe. A tall, lean man wearing a pinstripe navy suit stood beside it, his knee cocked, one arm cradling an oar. I was delighted to see that Buddy Holly was my captain—a fact demonstrated by his black horn-rimmed glasses—until I noticed he was not the lively young man I recalled from fast tunes and flashbulb pictures. He was emaciated and weathered, and the Pox had pitted his face. The Coke-bottle lenses of his glasses magnified tiny clouds of cataract. His hair was dull black, boot-polish dyed, and swept over in a pompadour, in a feeble attempt at fashion. But his suit—his suit was in tip-top condition! The pantleg creases were crisp and neat, and his wingtip shoes were polished to mirrory brightness. Only now did he speak:

> I like to show respect to passengers when I host their transportation. I bow and hum sing-song style when they step aboard. The smart ones bring gifts—a coin, a leaf made of hammered gold, an ivory trinket. When we hit open water, I play fiddle and blow a mouth harp and test my falsetto a cappello. I take requests from the passengers, but usually they're speechless. Not everyone is curious enough to embark on the Big Ship, and fewer still are willing to navigate the Major Divide in my agile low-draw canoe. But to think of recreation on the Far Shore is a different matter—death by dancing, nightlife fun and furor. I've seen the aged and the crippled stand upright and dance until dawn, all the while attracting bees like pollen and warm honey. I keep my suit immaculate; I iron it nightly. These old glasses are just for show—I was blinded a century ago, poked by an angry centaur brandishing a bamboo stick.

Buddy raised his arm, displaying a trembling St. Vitus hand. He flicked open his Steinway fingers suited for dizzying feats of bebop jazz and Bo Diddley syncopation. He reached inside his jacket and removed the baby-blue smartphone on which he kept the music. With one hand, he held the phone, with the other he gripped the oar—both shaking like nervous spiders. His voice dropped two octaves when he started humming. Imagine bass notes floating across the water in a loon's call of poignant glory. It must have been a loop, an ever-returning circle—the same few songs repeated time and again—because we stomped and sang and raved on for the full duration of a lifelong journey.[3]

Struck by Lightning

I was struck by lightning and mean to tell you about it. When I woke up, I caught the smell of something burning. My pant cuffs were singed, my zipper was welded shut. My face felt tender and my ears were ringing, and the fingers on my left hand were very sensitive. A lightning bolt had been tattooed on my left calf—it lasted two weeks before disappearing.[4] For a few days afterward I could feel the whole shape of whatever all at once just from gripping a part of it gently in my hand. My clothes and hair felt smooth and silky. When I first woke up and looked across the valley, it was filled like a bowl sloshing over, filled with nothing but empty space and air. It was late afternoon by then, the sky was entirely clear, the clouds had broken.

They told me that morning not to walk on the far side of the canyon. But I did anyway. It was steep, the rock was brittle and sandy and ready to crumble. I saw a storm churning the darkest sort of clouds and heard the sky rumbling but I couldn't leave the canyon, it was so beautiful. I went right ahead to the edge of the cliff, and it was there I was struck by lightning. It knocked me backward, otherwise I would fallen off the cliff and broken any number of bones. I was dead to the world, no telling how long. They call it a coma.

You might wonder what I saw there, what I didn't tell the doctor—he was the know-it-all type. His fountain pen with a little white cap must have cost fifty dollars. He said my IQ and memory had gone down and that I can't remember much of what I see. He said I had trouble reasoning when I needed to solve a problem using his red and white blocks. He said I might get lost driving or using maps. What his toys and blocks have to do with driving, I have no idea. He used a foreign word that sounded like bell-difference—it meant I didn't care about things and acted like everything was grand, like my mind worked just like it always had. He said I denied visions, which isn't half the story.

What I saw was light bright as day but soft and gentle. It didn't have a form unless stars have a form other than shine and brilliance. I felt something special I had felt only once or twice before, little tastes but nothing like the real thing. I wanted to stay there forever and melt like butter in a skillet. I was sizzling with love for something that had no shape. Since then, I read about leaving your body—you feel lightweight and carried along like floating on a river. I rose vertical, slowly at first, then faster, so fast I could have disappeared. But what happened instead was I woke up and felt nauseated, and I fell over when I tried to stand. I rested until I could make my way to the house. They drove me to the hospital. The doctor said the burns started at the right side of my neck and crossed over at my chest, then continued down to my left foot. They cut off my boots, ruined a new pair. My foot was red and swollen. The blisters eventually healed. This was six months ago, and since then I quit my job or got fired, the story runs both ways.

I haven't noticed much else except feeling different than before and hearing two kindly voices. One belongs to a boy, the other is a woman no older than me. They don't talk to me directly—they talk between themselves about me. They aren't exactly whispering, but the volume is low. I can barely make out what they say, it's so soft, never yelling. When I close my eyes before falling asleep, I see a faint picture of the light, and it's then the boy and woman are most talkative. I told a preacher about the lightning and he said I was like the apostle Paul. I read about Paul but couldn't understand what he meant. He was a long time ago, and now is a different world. I feel at ease and comfortable most all the time, like everything is alright. I could live under a bridge and not mind as long as I remembered the light and could hear those kindly voices.

The Celestial Jester

There was once a celestial jester, his nose a pig snout that flared like a trumpet bell. Stand-up bristles encircled the pink flesh at the snout's tip, and nappy tan fur ran lengthwise along its sides, ending where the snout joined the jester's cheeks. Here the tint and texture of the flesh were beautiful and lurid, its luxe pearly shine as inviting as a shark's belly. The jester's lips have the color of a ripe plum, and the peachy glow of his cheeks spans the entire horizon. He rarely opens his mouth and does so only at night. No one can say whether the jester's teeth are shiny clean or stained, square or pointed, if he has incisors or only a gaping set of molars. The jester's tongue is forked—a common opinion. Personal encounters create a squirming, billowing sensation and an anxious sense of dark limitless space. Queasiness, disgust, and moral revulsion are next to follow, and sometimes nausea and vertigo. The meaning of these feelings and the sickening visceral effects? Words are weakly reeds and brittle aspirations. They mean nothing when one stands face-to-face with evil.

The iris of the jester's eyes is lush brown, like wet moose hide, and dark enough to merge with the pupil. Not a landscape in the world gives as clear a feeling of rich fertile loam. Imagine the earth asleep, lolling in broad-breasted relaxation, when its most limpid dream rises visibly above the horizon. As wakefulness approaches, the dream's sense of coherence dissolves like rising vapor, meanwhile its emotional force grades into homogeneous uniformity, all nuances of difference disappearing. An ingratiating softening follows, a sweet tincture of forbidden wonder. This is the feeling of the lesson the jester's pupil learns from its lush brown iris.

The comb along the jester's head and neck is serrated and rooster-red. It has been mistaken for a lumberjack's saw spanning the dawn horizon. Children at play have seen stars aligned with the comb's jagged edge. Folk being folk, the comb has given rise to stories about a floppy crown, its protruding points stitched with bells. On this basis he acquired his name—the Jester.

Both scientists and folk have speculated about the jester's ears. Their ideas converge, collective fantasy gravitating toward a single image. The jester does not have external ears, the auricles found in mammals, but cartilaginous tubes that penetrate the inner table of his skull. Lizards, snakes, and frogs (and some toads and fish) are so equipped. The jester's earholes are protected by porous membranes, the tympana, which shield his brain from razor-sharp particles of stardust. An explorer who traveled widely in the African bush is an exception to an otherwise broad consensus. She said the jester does indeed have external ears—elephant ears, big as fluttering tent flaps. All agree, his hearing is acute, of such excellence that he can detect the rustle of windblown feathers on a sparrow's head.[5]

The jester's hair is black as a moonless night and falls in bouncy curls. Its beauty has provoked stories—a friend's girlhood experience is an example. Each night, paying strict attention to the images passing before her inner eye, she begrudged the fleeting parade of daytime residue, the specks of sensation and passing presences. All this activity, she said, was meaningless dross that must fall away before the fissioning center of her mind's most sheer and deep blackness appeared all about her, at which point she felt buoyant, as if swimming through the most nightly of nights. What others feared, she courted gingerly. She recounted the variable densities of blackness, the bounce and float of elongated forms. Curls unravelling by the dozen, all with the same bounce and float. Was this a curtain or was it a nighttime beach, the ease and swoosh of unfurling waves? Years later, hearing tales about the jester, she decided that what she saw as a girl was the unravelling of uncoiling hair.

Reported by a Respected Ethnographer

Our *Festschrift* honoring Henry Topos includes the present translation of a report he intended to deliver during the 1968 plenary session of the Conference on African Ethology. Topos's untimely death prevented his attending the conference, providing a translation, and preparing a scholarly apparatus. According to rumor, his paramour and research associate, Professor Anna Khoisan, leapt forward and beheaded the green-hooded viper that bit Topos as they crept along the dry Wanash riverbed in the desolate north-central Kalahari Desert. Topos died within hours from respiratory arrest and internal bleeding. The professor is renown for his ethnographic work among the Bushmen people living in that area. No other scholar has wasted as much ink on these backward natives and their primitive way of life. His unique and needless contribution has been to gather and translate dozens of the myths that comprise their oral tradition. Topos is recognized as the leading authority on their altogether strange "click" language. Late in his career, as Topos's dedication intensified, he smiled constantly and began speaking to his colleagues and students and his own wife exclusively in a Bushmen dialect. We are grateful to the professor's widow, Helga Topos, for permission to publish this last contribution of a distinguished career. We extend special appreciation to Professor Khoisan for translating Topos's otherwise unintelligible paper. The topic is a certain myth embraced by a little-known division of the Bushman people who inhabit the desolate northern region of present-day Namibia:

> The children of the tribal elders receive rigorous training in surviving for long periods without water. During their periodic migrations a band may wander for weeks without access to fresh water from either the oases that dot the dry bed of the Wanash River along the southern boundary of their migratory path or the springs that bubble from the volcanic rifts along the escarpment. The elders display remarkable ingenuity in pursuit of primitive technology designed for water conservation. The children are beneficiaries of such technology and the lore surrounding its creation. They are taught to view their bodies as supernatural

instruments for the conservation of liquid. Children undergoing the initiatory trials of puberty learn special techniques for inhibiting secretions and preserving for lengthy periods the water they drink. Natural bodily functions are trained: tears inhibited, mucous secretion suppressed, spitting forbidden, urination carefully monitored, ejaculation prohibited. Before commencing the migration, the children memorize a set of mythological beliefs unique in subequatorial Africa for its vivid images of an afterlife of lacustrine terrain governed by bibulous gods seated before spring-fed pools. The initiated are taught to view water preservation as a means of participating in afterlife. Perspiring, salivating, urinating and otherwise releasing liquid substances from the body bear sacramental importance. All naturally excreted liquid substances are exudates of the spiritual forces that perfuse afterlife and animate the bodies of the brave young tribesmen.

The most important legend of the tribe's stock of mythology concerns a boy living with his parents in an isolated encampment. The mother is dark as the night sky. Her mouth is likened to the new moon, her eyes are described as clusters of stars. The father is exquisitely agile and wiry as a reed, thin to the point of near-invisibility. The boy is portrayed as an awkward slow-witted buffoon. These characteristics of the family and particularly the absence of a maternal uncle have attracted the attention of several scholars, who find in these details justification for concluding that the parents are the primal couple—the mother and father of the first man. This first man is our buffoonish boy, a trickster figure, variously brilliant and foolish, who is tested and survives, and who becomes the proverbial spark of culture symbolized by his discovery of fire. The boy's power of autogenesis allows for self-regeneration after death. In primeval time he molded and fired the mud figurines that became the original tribal elders.

Returning to camp from a day's hunt the boy finds his parents' bodies a short distance from the family's thatched hut. They have died inexplicably. Their bodies are coated with a gray powder resembling ash and show no wounds or signs of injury. The spoor of a single bird encircles the bodies three times. The boy traces his parents' steps toward the hut and sees that their heel prints are not indented sufficiently to indicate the fear or panic of a sudden escape. Our slow-witted hero is numbed by the tragedy. He sits cross-legged and weeps, each tear lapped by his searching tongue. Taking account of his difficult circumstances he decides to walk to the camp of a neighboring tribe that lives on the far side of the desert. Preparing for flight he drinks the four gourds of water stored in the hut. He had never before drunk so much water at one sitting. He feels inundated, as expansive and full and deep as the blue ocean described in his parents' songs.

He begins at dusk, walking naked, traveling in the cool of night. Moving through vaporous moonlight he resembles a leaping shadow, a flitting moth. At daylight he crouches in the shade of dunes, motionless, hardly breathing. Years pass. His concentration never wavers. The boy grows into manhood with unwavering confidence in reaching his neighbors. He becomes as thin and wiry as his father. After years of travel his sole reminders of having a body are the friction of sand on his bare feet and the abrasive texture of wind on his face. Soon even these sensations fade. His mind is emptied, and soon after it vanishes. No one knows how long he wandered. There are numerous accounts, all alike in detail, which describe his arrival at the neighboring tribe's camp where he walked to the fire, paused, then peed and peed—at least four gourds worth.

Chandler, Hammett, and the Harrowing of Hell

A friend has sent a troubling report, its material properties more suitable for a wedding invitation than a description of horror. Engraved on stiff bond, the communication's every word is italicized. The handwritten note she enclosed in the same envelope says the report arrived by teletype—the outdated communication technology that produces a distinctive clacking sound while creating written documents. The rapid-fire clack-clack-clack features in noir fiction and in the movies and old radio dramas of the same genre. I had no difficulty recalling the noir world, its dark moral circumstances, shady characters, and famous practitioners. I enjoyed Simenon but favored the Americans—Raymond Chandler, whose detective Philip Marlowe navigates the sun-blanched highways of Los Angeles, and Dashiell Hammett, whose characters Sam Spade and the Continental Op track shadows through nighttime San Francisco.

I called immediately and arranged a visit. I was troubled by the noir invocation and worried about her safety. On several occasions during our thirty years of friendship, she had threatened suicide, the most noir of personal aggressions. Things in the outer world had darkened considerably since we last spoke—ubiquitous violence in word and deed, school shootings too numerous to list, financial markets imbued with the sanctity of holy sacraments, economic stratification rivaling the feudal era, gangs of Brown Shirts dominating chat rooms and patrolling the streets of major cities—not to mention imminent climate catastrophe. Medical societies warned of an epidemic of moral nausea: its symptoms of vertigo and vomiting result from the metabolic synergy of reading the news while eating breakfast. As a portent of worse to come, an obese queen—vain, hulking, effeminate—strides the world stage masquerading as a dictator. That a person of deep intuition and rich imagination might feel drawn toward noir nihilism was not surprising.

I saw her approaching a block away, navigating the foot traffic of a crowded San Francisco sidewalk. She stepped lightly, quickly, dodging other pedestrians, who gave no sign of noticing her presence mere inches away. No one turned, no one glanced or gave way, as if she were physically inconsequential, all but invisible. I recognized her leather jacket and skin-tight denim from our nightlife days. The emerald corduroy shirt was a new addition. We embraced for a few moments, simply folding into one another. I noticed a subtle perfume—something Southern, either magnolia or wisteria. Always thin, she was now rail-thin, which accentuated the structure of her face—the cheekbones, the high forehead, her lips compressed. Her hair was gray, no more than an inch in length. Hints of ageing were offset by a certain radiance. Her voice had become a rough-textured whisper. She put noticeable effort in enunciating every word—you might have thought English was not her native language. She still wore my grandmother's wedding band, a gift from years before, when our match was too obvious to draw comment from either one of us.

She explained the facts once we were seated and exchanged dilatory comments about the swans. Her report, she said, arrived by teletype during a lucid dream: "A polymodal experience, more convincing than any movie." She remembered every word and transcribed the entire report after awakening. "I first read it while dreaming—I saw it right before my eyes." Later, recalling the clacking sound, she thought of noir fiction and the radio programs she heard on her grandfather's big Zenith radio. Her report, she explained, is "an eye-witness vision of Hell," which she assured me is not her personal fantasy.

I sought additional information, enough to gauge her seriousness. I braved a query: "How dark are you willing to go?"

She answered immediately: "I enjoy an occasional fistfight and take pleasure in battering hustlers and liars with a putting iron. But I draw the line at homicide. The worst sort of violence is soul theft, a loss that adults can inflict on children. I spare no mercy in punishing its perpetrators."

She focused on the damage done to children: "Indigenous peoples have special knowledge about this sort of theft. Measures are taken to enforce a soul's return. Children's souls are the most vulnerable—blown off course as easily as a matchbox boat with a tissue-paper sail. People who steal children's souls are sent directly to Gehenna at death. Not a moment's pause—instantaneous metaphysical travel."

Her voice had become a barely audible whisper. She spoke of the hothouse Hell of Gehenna as if it were a place like any other—like Hawaii, Mississippi, or Sudan. My unease over her state of mind only increased when she claimed to have visited Hell and seen firsthand the naked bodies of child-killers punched through with tentacles of fire and flayed with knife-edged flames.

She assured me she felt certain about her report's every detail: "This report is a record of my visit to Gehenna, the Hell of soul thieves and child-killers, where Moloch bounces on tiptoes and swirls his barbed tongue along his victims' entrails. I saw naked men by the hundreds cut down like ripe wheat, falling before armies of razor scythes. I've seen all this, and now I understand—the psyche is a killing machine, and it will enforce its justice regardless of cost or delay. Blows will be counted, quotas of suffering calculated and administered. Scales will come into balance. The report you've confused with a wedding invitation is not a concocted tale—it is my itinerary."

She recounted the sound she heard during her nighttime vision of Gehenna. She heard clacking sounds while falling asleep, a series of hollow snaps. In trying to determine their origin, she remembered the cedar animal masks carved by the Kwakiutl people of the Pacific Northwest. She pictured Cannibal Raven, their wily trickster. The dancer's beak would open and shut in quick succession, emitting a clack-clack-clack. She had visited the tribe during an early pilgrimage and heard Cannibal Raven with her own ears.

Only later, after awakening, did she realize that the clacking sound mimicked teletypes: "I suppose it was inevitable I would remember the noir world, the old movies and radio programs. I devoured those books during college. I remembered Marlowe, the Continental Op, all those hard-boiled private detectives passing through crowded offices to fetch instructions and make calls on rotary-dial phones, meanwhile a dozen teletypes clacked like a platoon of hungry locusts. I remembered the dark alleys and steep brick streets, the Tiffany lamps and the green eyeshades, the hushed rendezvous steeped in silent pauses, the stiff faces shadowed by wide-brim fedoras. These men, the women too, sip rye whiskey from dinted flasks and remark on cigarette flares glimpsed two blocks away. Hammett's San Francisco was like my neighborhood as a girl. His high-society clients, in their vacuity and elegance and polished ease, were entirely familiar. I once shopped for a knee-length herringbone coat like a jacket worn by one of his characters."

She continued in this vein for several minutes before focusing on a particular visit to San Francisco: "Several years ago I visited the Mark Hopkins, at the top of Knob Hill. The height of old-world charm, this is the most luxe of the city's grand hotels. I was lured into the solarium by piano music shimmering with a Bill Evans patina. Couples were enjoying tea and drinking cocktails, seated at bistro tables in the indoor garden. A thin elderly man dressed in a tuxedo played a big Steinway with the elegant fingers of a born pianist. Stretched akimbo on the parquet at his side was a dark-haired young man of slight build dressed in white, a Pierrot figure in baggy pantaloons. I thought he was dead before noticing the beads of perspiration, his chest pumping from his racing breath. The scene triggered in me a sharp pang of sadness—I began to weep.

"I slipped past the concierges and the doormen and managed to dodge the hustling bellhops in their red tunics and brass buttons and jumping-monkey train-conductor hats. I walked across the park to the Gothic cathedral—I had wanted to pay homage to its icon of the jazz man John Coltrane. I found the painting suspended on a stone pillar, an ancient whipping post. Coltrane was bug-eyed—he looked stiff, stunned, afraid. He pressed the upright instrument against his chest like a parade flag. I suppose fear was the cost of blowing those flurries of exalted honks, meanwhile the drummer Elvin Jones rumbled like thundering Zeus, and pianist McCoy Tyner sculpted blocks of color with his mighty left hand. Coltrane's sax was formed of tamped gold leaf—it burned like a torch in the cathedral's smudged candlelight."

By now my friend's face was still and vacant as if she were wearing a mask. I snapped my fingers beside her ear without eliciting a blink. I read her report aloud as we sat together face-to-face:

> I see a leaden sky pressing on pock-marked plains—crevices opening, magma rising, decimated fields and scattered brush fires. Buffeting gusts blow from opposite directions, raising columns of grit. Bulging tubas pulse in erratic beats. Legs, arms, and tangled viscera swim through the air like shoals of fish. The buzz of punched tambourines sizzles within burlesque tunes pumped from a battered accordion. Women clutching headless babies shout in peacock voices while stomping on mounds of daffodils. Spooked children twist hurdy-gurdy cranks.
>
> The men have formed opposing camps—those with dollar signs marked on their foreheads are dancing naked, impervious to the heat; the others, dressed in threadbare suits, hop in circles, jangling sistrums and neighing in hee-haw donkey fashion. The men toss rocks and heave spears, rarely taking aim. Stumbling, flailing, they shout orders at every step.

Hundreds of black briefcases have taken flight and begun to congregate in ominous murmurations. The air is noxious, a combination of acetone, marigolds, and rotting meat.

Shuffling crowds gasp and cry, plunge and fall, strangled and coiled, ivy sprouting from every orifice. Hordes of two-dimensional forms advance in cartoon fashion, throwing gang signs and prancing with accentuated hipness. The ground beneath their feet momentarily becomes transparent. Farther down, I see eroded human forms standing chest-deep in a slurry of ice. Blue sparks of burning acetylene flash across its surface. Their mouths are black apertures round as circles. I hear wheezy cries and bass-note moans sustained for seconds, all in monotone.

See the autocracy of Hell, the tastemakers of our carrion race—the money titans, the tech barons, the barking hyenas, the crazed capuchin monkeys banging on their media cells, and the big-muscle buffalo men now reduced to mincing toddlers. Twittering harpies fill the sky—I mistake them for exploding exclamation marks until their screams fill my ears.

I pause, swayed by pulses of despair, before hearing whispered messages channeling the stealth of kindness. I couldn't say what other sound I heard—its tonal quality was confounding. Cooing dove or mewling babies, but mostly it recalled the bone-hollow tapping of bamboo swept with autumn breeze.

Draperies blue as night unfurl across the horizon. Such lovely stars, and the moon quickly waxing toward fullness. At the farthest stretch of the evening's dimming light, I see a line of pennants twinkling red and white, an arrow of fluttering lights passing straight through the storm.

I look up from reading to see my friend attentive and fully awake, her smile as warm as I remember from our days at school. She had become my detective, the dark operative of metaphysical travel. For reasons I couldn't understand, I pictured that ancient sculpture of the nighttime goddess standing bolt upright on her eagle-talon feet. I was no longer worried about her safety. Intrepid and subtle, she had tested the limit of visionary power and returned to deliver a firsthand report. She could induce her own absence and just as easily restore her presence. Her power was the resilience hidden in her disappearing act.[6]

4. Unusual Bodies

The Train

Beside the rails when chiming bells and crossbars flashing announce a roar I will in time absorb. With me now three engines pounding, the deafening noise growing louder. Pulled to the clamor of metal aching and engines pounding, enveloped in the roar of clacking cars and metal bending, I am open and free to dance, a dry leaf succumbing to wind, the dust enhanced by skipping and hopping, my partner counting beats at dozens of wheels.

Remember the Summer

"Take me!" he whispered, repeating the exclamation three times over, meanwhile drawing closer. Amazed, then awed, he saw the figure did not cast a shadow. Light unlike the sun or the moon, different than any known luminosity. Impossibly brilliant, impossibly soft, and gentle beyond all expectations. To bask in the light, melting into its aura, irradiated by the presence. Death would have been a fair trade—the boy would have preferred to die. They called one to the other in the breezy cool of evening. Few summons carry equal strain or equal certainty. How to say *love* when words have been reduced to motes swimming in dead air? Perfect virtue is struck from the mold of the luminous figure. Conscience is a mite compared with its demands. He knew its wishes both particular and general, its perfect demands. How to tell people that burning solace awaits them? How to apply the balm that singes? To have the figure nearby was terrible. Its withdrawal stirred grief over the gaping absence. This is the blessing that curses.

Smiles Modest as Ripe Wheat

(1) Rising from a roiling vein of liquid silver is a boy whose chest, head, and upraised arms shine with beads of saltwater. His eye sockets are shadowed, tentacles of matted hair wreathe his skull. He is rising, a glistening form now blurred. At the peak of his lilt, I shut my eyes, and laden with the image of his transfiguration I am submerged beneath the waves.

(2) The boy is parading his famous nostalgia and invites me to join him on the shore. Banners, tents and breeze, fishing boats in the offing. Unescorted women fetching shells at low tide. Alone on the shore with the boy, hand-in-hand, smiles modest as ripe wheat awaiting the kiss of the scythe.

Four Stems, Multiple Blooms

Four stems, multiple blooms, braced against the lip of the water glass. Each a delicate vice, a pale reminder of earth's fresh start. Plucked just yesterday and set to breathe on the kitchen counter tended by the plump hands of the Baptist divorcée. There were five at lunch: the jowly Baptist and her canary daughter, an elderly widow, and a fourth woman, ripely middle-aged and saddled with a housebound mate. I cleared dishes, helping our hostess, who pressed her face to the scent as I raised mine.

"Narcissus!" she said. "Aren't they lovely?"

To which I replied, "Oh, yes! I hadn't known the name," nor the source of the sweetness that veiled her pungency.

Gazing Woman

She gazed at the freshly curling hair inside the boy's thigh. He stood to her side, mounted on a stepladder, her head level with his waist. The caged green finch perched nearby. Raising the water pitcher, he touched the rim of its dish. After withdrawing the spout, he pulled aside, his face lined in the striped shadow of the backlit cage. A moment later, she turned and spoke, her voice needlessly cadent and unusually strained as she lingered in the backdraft of a body plummeting toward the secluded pond where her eyes were already floating. Her eyes—lidless globes marveling at the quaking iridescence of a pitch-black sky.

Enveloped

Instantly enveloped in a voluminous scarf of the finest silk—a single garment running head-to-foot, impossibly sheer, billowing toward the objects to which he attended. His perceptual reach was transformed simultaneously with this startling change of awareness: distance shrunk in proportion to the expansion of his presence. His grasp, quick as his perception. He touched objects in anticipation of his fingers' contact, and each conformed perfectly with his touch. Darts of super-acute sensibility were plain and obvious. Shifts of scale occurred instantaneously. The marble cigarette case resting on the nearby table was translucent to the wisps of agate-colored clouds embedded in its cool, slick surface. The seam where the lid met the case, no thicker than a pencil line, appeared as wide as a highway. The embossed crease where the case heaved its weight against the leather tabletop was spacious as a canyon. Had he been these objects, they could not have known a more delicate touch. Had he been himself, they would have been clumsy implements worked by awkward hands.

Ball Bearing

Adrift on a spring night, her manicured body bound and folded. The rhythmic snap of the cobbled street, a dozen windows mirrored in the glassy sheen of puddled rainwater. Her hips' sway tracks the notched amplitude of genteel readiness. Flushed poise engorged with wishes. Draped silk and fingered stockings rubbing with the parched tone of fine sandpaper. Itchy steps traversing coarse pavement, her pining gait scratching the packed surface of a hidden beach. Turning in perfect rotations, her furled umbrella held bolt upright, a silver ball balanced precisely on the tip of its spine.[7]

Full Disclosure

When things around you pass into full disclosure and the space between them is no different than the things themselves—when the shininess begins, a patterned array in motion, then it's all new and you have been invaded. Roofs collapse, walls tremble, a barbell is pumped in heaven. Every hand has become an open palm and fists are now forbidden. Surely you see, you must see, your status has changed. You can speak for the patterned array. Each thing stands on intimate terms with its neighbors when you give it direction. But now a decision must be made right away, prolonged ambivalence is intolerable: either retreat or pass into the smithery array. Greet the day or pass away. What do I say? Courage is a fool's delight this tipsy world will bring to ruin. Evade the din! Muffle the cymbals! Escape is the prudent face of valor.

Charged and Sprawled

I reject wrestlers, baseball caps, and oilskin dusters. The fatuous bragga-docio of native-born vacancy makes me sick. I reject blue-suit fathers and keening beefsteak sons. Enough of these flap-jack yokels and tricked-out prophets basking in manly chuckles! I reject their ceaseless hurrahs and gluttonous avarice. Bivalve hearts, serpent tongues—windbags of sentimen-tality! None is quick or rose-bedecked. None can see my self-concatenating extension across open space. I stand empty, face-to-face.

I am the armed-drone slayer of maximum ugliness. I explode armored cars and pummel gassy high horses. I direct crushing firepower at the cheap shadows of commercial logic. I wreck the veneer and raise the rubble to charred altars in high-court heavens. Hear the pounding resonance of a cavernous beat rattling tin-roof skies.

> Sing-song little lamb.
> Hoppity-loppity bunny
>   bouncing down the forest trail.
> Oh Humpty, dear Dumpty, where is your crown?
> Scattered shards litter the ground.

I am the blue dragonfly sizzling on red-hot coals. I am the black-loam eye of the deep-ocean albatross. I am the drift and haze of butterfly wings dis-pensing puffs of zircon pollen. Walk with me and the migrating caribou beneath shimmering ceilings of sap-green auroras.

I reject the net, tighten the wire, and sprinkle talcum on my slippers. I am a divine nimbus of hammered gold formed of fierce attraction. I crush the stellar grid of ruinous destiny. I snap the Graces' beaded cord and celebrate its unravelling.

I am charged and sprawled, atomized, a helpless vapor. A dancing fool—a witless fly, I can barely dodge the swatter. Leave me adrift in shifting clefts of rising tides, lounging beside fresh bodies resting on tendrils of straw-blond wheat, and forever protected from the sadness of leaving—meanwhile, all the while, standing stock-still, sniffing the salt air blown from my grandfather's greenhouse fan.[8]

5. Eye of the Circle

Monsieur Teste

Paul Valéry portrays his famous character Monsieur Teste as a "man of incomparable mental gymnastics," a paragon of "pure intellect."[9] Many of his descriptions of Teste could pass as autobiographical fragments. The two men are similar; in certain respects, identical. Valéry and his character breathe the common air of precise luminous mentation. Teste's precision of mind redounds to Valéry, a self-acknowledged mathematician of versification. Valéry tracks Teste—Teste shadows Valéry. A pictorial analogy of their relationship is Escher's lithograph "Drawing Hands," in which each hand of the pair draws the details that complete the other. Absent reciprocal aid, neither Valéry (the writer) nor Teste (the character) would have come to completion. Their close resemblance justifies a question: Is Teste the antecedent of Valéry, the agent that caused the writer to reproduce the character? I suppose the writer materialized while describing his character. But Teste is the more hazardous and chilling of the two men. He has precedence, and he stands in relation to Valéry in the way that sculptural figures spoke to Michelangelo while they slept in gray-veined blocks of milky Carrara marble.

Valéry and Teste meet outdoors and indoors, in cafes and on the street. Valéry spies Teste seated in a box seat at the theatre, strangely backlit as if he were a malign spirit. He sees him standing beside a golden column in the mezzanine at the opera—alert, observant, unnoticed. Valéry and Teste stroll the boulevards of Paris during the fading glories of the Belle Époque and, later, after the First World War had ravaged optimism. Valéry listens to Teste's ruminations and precise descriptions as he falls asleep, raked with physical pains in a gray claustrophobic hotel room.

Valéry was acquainted with Teste's wife, Emilie, and shares with readers her correspondence about her husband. Valéry says little about Teste's everyday activities and livelihood apart from referring to his "frugal weekly speculations on the stock market." His descriptions of Teste's physical appearance are similarly sparse: "Monsieur Teste was perhaps forty years old. His speech was extraordinarily rapid, and his voice low. Everything about him was unobtrusive, his eyes, his hands. Yet his shoulders were military and his step had an astonishing regularity."

Teste's birth coincided with dire events in Valéry's personal life: simultaneous crises of vocation, romance, and intellectual direction.[10] Valéry likens the struggles of this period to "mental martyrdom" and the political revolution and coup d'état that hastened Napoleon Bonaparte to power. He sketched the related details in the autobiography he wrote decades later:[11]

> I returned home from my third year of law.
> All the preceding *themes* were aggravated.
> I could write poetry only with great difficulty. A love affair finished me.
> Finally, having taken my law degree—and just barely—I went to spend a month in Italy, where I suffered an acute mental martyrdom. Despair in every direction. Extra-lucid nights.
> And I passed through my inner 18 Brumaire which led to the advent of "Mr. Teste."
> This meant that I resolved to think with rigor—to *not believe*—to consider as null and void everything that could not be brought to total precision, etc.

Teste's advent coincided with Valéry's dedication to rigorous thinking, when he "set about looking into the exact sciences . . . and studied mathematics, but in a very odd spirit, as a *model* of acts of the mind." At the time, Teste and his creator were reciprocally related: the coherence and precision of Teste's mind compensated for the upheaval and turbidity in Valéry's.

Arriving in Paris as a young man, Valéry began to attend the weekly Tuesday salon of his literary mentor, the symbolist poet Stéphane Mallarmé. He dedicated years of morning labor to writing his *Cahiers*, his personal notebooks, which have drawn nearly as much critical attention as his poetry and essays. Valéry represented France at the League of Nations. In 1925, he was elected to the Académie Française. He was nominated for the Nobel Prize on a dozen occasions, by such luminaries as Bergson, Poincaré, and the entire Académie Française. Apart from his literary work, I suppose Valéry was the first public intellectual of the modernist period. He died in 1945, and after receding from critical attention he has lately assumed a position of prominence. New translations of Valéry's work have begun to appear: *Monsieur Teste*, in 2024; a collection of prose and verse, published in 2021; and, in 2024, a bilingual edition of his collected verse appeared in the Oxford World's Classics series. [12]

Teste engaged Valéry's attention for his entire adult life, beginning with the 1896 publication of *La Soirée avec Monsieur Teste*. What remained unpublished of the Teste cycle at the author's death was published soon after. The one exception is *Eye of the Circle*, a work of indeterminate genre that Valéry attributed to Teste. I discovered this piece in manuscript form, boxed and shelved among Valéry's *Cahiers* in the Bibliothèque Nationale de France. How it remained hidden until its discovery in 2013, I cannot say, except to remark that the *Cahiers* are voluminous, spread over thirty thousand pages. *Eye of the Circle*, only a few pages in length, could easily have been overlooked.

I begin with an analysis of Teste's character and talents. An introduction of this nature is essential, otherwise *Eye of the Circle* would remain obscure, all but impenetrable. I next discuss the piece itself and provide a translation. Finally, I bear down on the difficulties in interpreting *Eye of the Circle* and determining Valéry's true purpose in writing it. Quoted material is cited in the endnotes. I retain Valéry's ellipses, emphases, and line breaks throughout.

TESTE'S CHARACTER AND TALENTS

Teste operates at the outer margin of the knowable—his natural habitat is endgames. He slays absurdities and incinerates dross. His daily project is "the continual practice of extreme conditions and critical phases of thought." As "a man of precision and vivid distinctions," he "never said anything *vague*." Teste is the Aztec priest's green obsidian blade—an elegant means of sacrifice.[13] Exercising a special "talent for *transcendence*," he lifts the "strange carnival" of everyday life into "excesses of abstraction" and "ventures far beyond ordinary time." Teste is an exact orchid, the ideal specimen cultivated in Enlightenment-era soil.

Analysis is not his only aim—meditative influx is another. "A bit more of such absorption," remarks his wife, "and I am sure that he would be invisible." Intellectual excellence can sap personal color and register as blandness of appearance. So it is with Teste, who is ashen on cloudy days and imbued with a pearly luster on moonless nights. His dull suits and inconspicuous demeanor, his near-invisibility in crowds, disguise megaton bursts of brilliance.

Teste's stated goal is "to work out my whole thought" and by such means to arrive at "the very end of me." He recognizes his plan's futility because he has already "arrived at that strange state of being unable to regard his own decision or inner response as more than an expedient, knowing very well that his thought would go on endlessly and that the idea of *ending* no longer has any meaning in a mind that knows itself well enough." Thought proceeding endlessly, the very idea of *ending* having lost meaning: so Valéry describes Teste's mental freedom, his intellectual facility, his ease of movement in mental space.

Teste's talents and practices are not the result of his personal history or physical constitution. Nothing superior to his own mind dictates its operation. He rejects ideas that endorse or hint of destiny or fate, and similarly avoids the baited hooks of temperament and character. Such ideas presuppose some form of predetermination, which Teste wholly rejects. Presuppositions that devolve from absolutes are instantly subject to his critique—"God," "self," and "soul" included. Teste has no time for daimons, fate, or endless flux—he is an enemy of Heraclitus.[14] His mind is the pristine site of his "purely ideal experiments."

Teste is a maestro of perceptual phenomena. He illuminates moments of mental activity at their points of inception. He can magnify the infinitesimal and miniaturize the enormous. Barely detectable sensory phenomena bloom under his powers of observation: "Not an atom escaped him of all that was becoming perceptible." For Teste, butterfly wings in motion have the timbre of a clapped encore in a crowded theatre.

Teste is porous to the aggressive tactile ambitions of the physical world, those of his own body included. Emilie speaks of his impassioned clasp-knife grip, the decisive firmness of his touch, his "exquisite and surprising gentleness."[15] Teste's examination of physical pain is as precise as his study of marginally apparent perceptual phenomena. Slipping beneath his bedtime covers, he describes wave-like aches welling into seascapes of discomfort:

> This is very odd. Suddenly, I can see into myself . . . I can make out the depths of the layers of my flesh; I feel zones of pain . . . rings, poles, plumes of pain. Do you see these living forms, this geometry of my suffering? There are certain flashes that are exactly like ideas.

Teste's bedtime scrutiny of aches and pains demonstrate his introspective search for an ultimate principle—a most basic mediating operation that brings phenomena before the conscious mind.

Teste displays curiosity and blunt objectivity and a certain calculating animosity toward the body, his own body, as might a laboratory scientist examining an experimental subject. The body, in its "its physical nature," imposes "conditions" that impede his introspective search for "the pure or absolute Me."[16] This same Me is "identical in us all, rejects all, is opposed to all." Teste characterizes this Me as "Zero" and calls it "the nexus of sensibility and 'consciousness.'" These themes appear elsewhere in *Monsieur Teste*, as when Valéry writes:

> He is *beside* his body and his fate, and he is of his [own personal] milieu.
> Before any reflection he is a particular sensation: need, pain, caution. And at the furthest point of reflection, he rejects *everything* (or there is total rejection). *Pure Self.*

Valéry's brevity is counterproductive. His final sentences can be summed and rewritten, the better to show his intent: At the severe extreme of his interior reflection and analysis, Teste finds that all phenomena, the whole world of personal experience, falls away, at which point he exposes the pure Self—the central, unadulterated, most fundamental cognitive function.

Teste's appearances in social settings are not dominated by the constraints of etiquette. His persona is a trapdoor disappearing act, a feat of legerdemain that erases its own occurrence. "He never smiled, nor said good morning or goodnight." He "seemed not to hear a 'How are you?'" When speaking he "never lifted an arm or a finger; he had *killed his puppet*"—the socially constructed *I*, the source of idiosyncratic personal static, the marionette of the face-to-face:

> In short, he had replaced the vague notion of the self that falsifies all our reckonings and slyly involves us in our own speculations—who are trapped in them—by a definite imaginary being, a well-defined or trained Self, precise as an instrument, sensitive as an animal, and adaptable to everything.

Having spent an entire evening with Teste, Valéry mused: "What had he done with his personality?"

Valéry calls Teste "the witness" and "the man of glass." The pairing is consequential and probably dialectical. Teste sees and is seen, each to an extreme degree. Only amplify the paired qualities and Teste-the-seen-through-man-of-glass becomes invisible, as if socially nonexistent, while Teste-the-witness becomes all-seeing, like an omniscient god. His status as the man-of-glass promotes friction-free passage through the social world—no snags, barriers, or burrs of embarrassment that might ruffle his ease.

Teste is a subdued bystander amid the bustle. After strolling and dining with Teste one evening, Valéry remarks, "I noticed that no one paid him any attention." Meanwhile, Teste's status as all-seeing witness implies that his gaze is comprehensive and the objects to which he attends are fully absorbed; no remainder. He says as much: "I sacrifice myself inwardly to what I would be!"—indicating absorption and assimilation. He is suited for such experiments because his mental powers do not cohere into a single vital center. Poised in the mode of observation, Teste provides ease of ingress to foreign bodies.

Teste is a placid mimic who neither seeks nor attracts attention. He is the arithmetical average of his ambient environment. Observed while idling in a grocery queue or standing in a police line-up, he would appear the same as his neighbors. "I hate extraordinary things," he remarks. "I am at home in MYSELF." What sort of home might this be—a temporary encampment, an anchorite's cave, surely not a stately mansion? Valéry once asked Teste: "What do you do all day?" His response: "I invent myself." His inventiveness entails an elasticity of personality, a hair-trigger readiness to slip the bonds. Its operation converges with emotional detachment and the fluency of intellectual genius.[17]

Strolling among his fellow humans, Teste finds that their "mechanisms are revealed to a certain look"—his own look, his objective gaze. It is not their subjective qualities that hold his attention but "their physiological and social time-tables—their daily or secular growth." The point is clear: "Monsieur Teste in such a setting would feel himself surrounded by automatons." In other words, depersonalization has become a way of life, Teste's gambit when entering the *mise en scène* of others.

One of Teste's peculiar skills is to nap while awake. In this manner, he surpasses a division that other persons are compelled to obey. Draping a scrupulous skein of attention over his subliminal psyche, he sidles through its teeming pools, its moody troughs and crests of meaning. "I am fond of navigating the night," he once remarked. No dark twist of mind remains that might hinder or distort his self-perception: "I see through myself from the farthest end of the world down to my unspoken word."

Teste is a polymath without competitiveness, pretensions, or a compulsion to talk. His conversational repertoire excludes sarcasm and darts of irony. He has no appetite for either small talk or written texts:

> I gave up books twenty years ago. I have burned my papers also. I scrape the quick... I keep what I want. But that is not the difficulty.

It is rather to keep what I shall want tomorrow . . . I have tried to invent a mechanical sieve.

Writing, much less publishing, hold no interest: "Neither was he a philosopher, nor anything of that kind, nor even a writer; and for that reason, he thought a great deal—for the more one writes, the less one thinks." In conversation with Valéry, Teste remarks: "Erudition and collecting, signs of impotence. They don't understand that works are waste products, excrement." Teste seeks instantaneous, fully formed moments of clarity, not their dull, delayed residue in writing or collections: "Knowledge despises what cannot be circumscribed in an instant."

Teste "was born of chance." Valéry insists on the point and stresses its importance: "All the mind he has or had comes from this fact." Teste's chance-born status is the source of his objectivity and intellectual facility. His mental capacity is freely determined, not a by-product of character, history, or constitutional inheritance. And, born of chance, Teste can navigate the sea of chance whose tides move through everyday life. He is a placeholder in a chain of accidents: "There is in me some faculty, more or less active, to consider—and it even *must* consider—my tastes and distastes as purely accidental."

Teste's mental freedom is not a believable state of affairs. His freedom is Valéry's aspiration for his character, his wish in portraying a figure of maximum solipsistic independence. The pure creature of chance is merely a dream of freedom—a navy beret suspended in a cloud of Gauloises smoke.[18] The very idea contradicts the fact of natural determinants; corkscrew spirals of genetic material being a leading example. Valéry needs his character to fit such a description because Teste's chance-born status ensures (we are told) the superior and superbly unbiased quality of his thinking. What passes in Teste's mind appears in high relief, perfectly nuanced. His detachment and freedom guarantee these effects and erase what remains of any feeling of pride. Teste and pride are incommensurable. As Valéry remarks, it was only after he reached "a rather mature age" that Teste was "in the least aware of the *singularity* of his mind."

Teste's mind is a transformative medium, an alembic, "the most complete psychic transformer, no doubt, that ever was." He "carries dissociation, substitution, and similitude to the extreme, but [remains] sure of recovery, an infallible operation." Teste reconstitutes himself with ease following moments of self-dissolution: "He always recovered from it the richer."

His mental talents lead Teste to a belief in the wholly comprehensive reach of his mind: "Everything seemed to him a special case of his mental functioning, and the functioning itself . . . identical with the idea or sense he had of it." All that passes passes within his mind—apart from a certain unavoidable exception: "At the end of the mind, the body." Here, then, solipsism crumbles. So enters pain, the limit and bogeyman of Teste's universe. Teste discusses pain in flat uneventful prose, his own pain included:

> Pain is due to consciousness and its resistance to some local disposition of the body. A pain we could clearly conceive and almost circumscribe would become a sensation without pain; and we might, in that way, come to know something directly about our deeper body, a knowledge on the order of that we find in music. Pain is something very musical, we can almost talk about it in musical terms.

Teste's prose begins to lapse, its tension to dissipate, as he works the analogy to music. The result is a countdown of desiccated metaphors: "Certain pains are grave and acute, some andante and furioso, held notes, organ stops, arpeggios, progressions, sudden silences, etc." Would it not be obscene (in a moral sense) to call the suffering of cancer a symphony of pain, a *Rite of Spring* in which Nijinsky's leaps represent evanescent attempts to evade the inevitability of death?

The imposition of pain highlights the strains and occasional agonies of everyday life:

> Teste is painfully present, a pain entirely contrary to his essence, in the important effort of his will to be a witness against the infernal power of the body *b*, and the world *w*, and, above all, of the inner reaction of the mind *m*.

Valéry's symbols—*b*, *w*, *m*—create a charade of formulaic exactness. Their use is simply aspirational, and yet the underlying point is important: Teste is "painfully present," unavoidably so, based on the aims and overreach of his will, "his will to be a witness," his intent to stand over and against the "power of the body . . . the world . . . and, above all, the inner reaction of [his own] mind." He assumes that his deepest discomforts are "searching for a mechanism that might . . . convert pain into knowledge."

Teste's remarks about death occur under the heading "End of Monsieur Teste." Valéry invokes a trace of ironic humor in concluding as follows: "Intellect's end. Funeral march of thoughts." The scene is dramatic but emotionally parched. Lying in bed, apparently in pain, Teste says:

> Goodbye. Soon a certain way of seeing will . . . end . . . Perhaps suddenly, now! Maybe tonight in a gradual decline, little by little unaware of itself . . . Yet I've worked all my life toward this minute.
>
> After a while, perhaps, before the end, I shall have that important instant—and perhaps grasp the whole of myself in one terrible look. Not possible.
>
> Syllogisms falsified by suffering, a stream of joyous images bathed in pain, fear mingled with happy moments of the past.
>
> And yet, what a temptation death is.
>
> Something unimaginable enters the mind in forms of desire and horror in turn.

"I've worked all my life toward this minute," Teste reports, referring to the passage to death. Since Plato's *Phaedo*, philosophical analysis has been interpreted as death's enquiring twin. Notice the stark vocabulary: terrible, suffering, pain, fear, desire, and horror—words that signal a troubled end and none of the abstraction and elevation that comes so naturally to Teste. The writer and his character invoke a brave face in meeting the bookend null states of personal death and pre-birth absence. Life, in Teste's words, is "a matter of going from zero to zero . . . From unconsciousness and insensibility to unconsciousness and insensibility."

Teste recognizes the operative force of words: "What one *can do* with *words*. That is everything." He acknowledges an aspiration to escape language altogether, on which basis he could see every object in its absolute novelty. Teste, a wordless observer, seeks "the stranger's way of looking at things, the eye of a man who *does not recognize*, who is beyond this world, the eye as frontier between being and nonbeing—belongs to the *thinker*." The perspective of Teste's thinker is like "the eye of a dying man, a man losing recognition." As such, everything shines with novelty.

Teste's diary entries are scattered like breadcrumbs throughout Valéry's *Cahiers*. Elusive tidbits, some are unintelligible. I have tracked Teste's loping spoor across nameless deserts and tiptoed in close pursuit along the scimitar arcs of perfect barchans. He taps my shoulder. He mumbles in my ear, transmitting comedy and poignance and strange associations:

> "Flat water has no fizz. A child's bubble bath is sad in the way of a zoo."[19]

"Peering within, hardly a barrier in sight, I see two gnats, a tattered winglet of *Drosophila*, the faint outline of an exclamation mark.[20] Might I say, I am glass."

"The alphabet—a set of letters of varied shapes. Dangling, fixed, and some protruding like tonsils. Many are paired: morphemes become phonemes, either bound or free. The bound variety combines two letters, creating an elemental sound. 'Hoot' said the owl. 'Toot' said the boy. Tonsils—two per set, either tubal or palatine. Paired and dangling, like testicles. Similar problems, the lexical mimicking the anatomical and medical: for example, the tonsillitis of semantic inflammation. Symptoms: loquaciousness and the terrible disease of extraneous meaning. Spare me superfluous nouns! Treatment is indicated: pharyngeal extrication—castration, severing bluster and throttled chuckles."

"Pass the forceps, sniff the ether. 'Go easy and relax, my little titan! Remove those tights and the bellwether tutu. Slip off those lace-up Oxfords with the patent Spanish heals.'"

MONSIEUR TESTE'S *EYE OF THE CIRCLE*

The training exercise described in *Eye of the Circle* demonstrates the mercurial, shape-shifting nature of the human body. I refer to the lived body, the somatic entity whose animating center is the incarnate self. The lived body is the personally enlivened body—the humanly configured form that mediates direct experience of life. It differs from the "two-legged form," which is Teste's name for the physical organism, the body palpated by physicians, shuttled through imaging devices, scrubbed with soap and water, bruised in car crashes, pummeled on the playground, and dressed in clothes of certain measurements. In the course of everyday life, the lived body and the two-legged form are isomorphic and mutually responsive. But the ease and congeniality of their relationship is tenuous and easily disrupted, and largely dependent on health, wakefulness, and sobriety. The convergence of the two bodies represents an elusive truce among territorial factions.

The lived body has sufficient power to cast off two-legged fetters and impose sudden perceptual changes in the affected person's sense of weight, size, shape, and position. The stability that imbues the two-legged form melts away when the lived body escapes its normal constraints and behaves like a bird in flight and a criminal fleeing captivity. Examples are common in dreaming and intoxication and during carnal relations. Lightning strikes of eros surge through the two-legged form, imposing downstream effects on the lived body. Sex is a magic act—a wonderworking dysmorphophobia that transforms the lived body into a knotted variant of its calmer shape. The masculine aspect of this unsettling drama is a pumpjack of exertions. The corresponding feminine metaphors derive from meteorology, seismography, and plate tectonics rather than the mechanics of drill bits and petroleum engineering.

Practiced vigorously and diligently, Teste's routine of mental training results in an extraordinary perception of self-expansion. The affected person's lived body is transformed into a virtually palpable field of conscious awareness, homogenous throughout. Ambient space has become the content of perception; the objects that populated it have melted away. Because the newly formed spatial field surrounds the two-legged form, Teste calls it "circumambient." He says nothing about corresponding emotional effects. I suppose they can be imagined as a wondrous feeling of unconstrained freedom.[21]

The manuscript of *Eye of the Circle* was free of corruption at the point of its discovery, apart from the final paragraphs where Valéry's crosshatched erasures had torn the page. His crude drawings of stars and stick figures along the right-hand margin were made with such pressure that the paper appears as if it were embossed. Three handwritten lines near the bottom of the final page slant from the horizontal and intertwine, creating an unbroken weave that terminates in a nearly illegible knot of letters. This odd effect, known to paleographers as the *textual braid*, is first reported in ancient Coptic papyri, specifically in recitation formulae that infuse amulets with magical power based on the thaumaturgy of women's hairstyles. Valéry sets off the several, very brief concluding paragraphs with a series of three hand-drawn stars, which I reproduce as asterisks.

Eye of the Circle

Your enemy throughout this exercise is mental clutter—the busy mind echoing the noise and bustle of the business of life. Seek vigilance. Cultivate purity of attention. In moments of slippage, return immediately to baseline alertness. I present the method in an outdoor setting, as when I first executed it successfully. Modifications will be needed to suit different training circumstances.

Attend to your location, the exact spot where you are standing. Sense the pressure gravity exerts on the soles of your feet. Register the surrounding details: forms, colors, the rounded dome of the sky, any curvature of the landscape. Once you feel thoroughly familiar with the scene, alter your strategy and begin to scan the landscape, proceeding quickly and repeatedly. Inhabit your eyes, pay attention as they rotate in panning movements. A disc of undisturbed space surrounds your location: quiet and still, not a blade of grass so much as nodding. Beyond this nearer band of space is a second panorama marked by the windswept face of the encircling hills: grass bent under gentle pressure; a bird braced in midflight. Tracks of breeze can be seen running through distant trees, mimicking rolling surf. The gentle tumult of the second panorama contains the quiescent nearer landscape. The band of space that most immediately surrounds your body is set within a horizon defined by the windswept motion of the distant hills.

As you see, a certain geometric arrangement has come into play: two concentric bands of space surround the fixed center where your two-legged form is situated. The nearer bands rests within a more distant band, and the distant band extends outward from the hills that mark the nearer band's outer margin. This is the very moment for which you have waited—the perfect circumstance: a means of cultivating an extraordinary perception in which you expand beyond your two-legged form and fill the disc of space encircling your location.

Survey the nearer band of space with brief, quickly administered glances. Attend to its circumference, its outer margin, which forms the inner border of the more distant field of space. Avoid lingering while you cast darts of attention like bow-shot arrows aimed all along the circumference. Advance point-to-point, rapidly and decisively. Continue just so, and eventually you will notice a subtle, stunning, momentary surprise: you have spanned the scene—you occupy two places at once. This recognition arrives in the mode of immediate retrospect. The linear extent of your expanded presence is indicated by the endpoints of the imaginary vector that spans your two-legged form and the inside rim of the quiescent panorama in the distance. The encircling band of space has been cut by a momentarily detectable radius. Based on your experience of the newly established vector, this same success can be repeated time and again.

Now that you have sliced the encircling band, you are primed to embody it. Remain steady, dead-center, the axial point of the surrounding landscape, while populating the circumference of the encircling band of space with rapidly placed points of attention, each point representing the target of a single act of displacement in which your attention darts outward and touches the rim. Speedily and efficiently, drawing on maximum alertness, direct your attention to successive points along the circumference you split when first attending to the band of space encircling your two-legged form. Many darts will be needed, possibly dozens. Initially, situate the points in close formation, one and then another, each located in proximity to its neighbors front and back. Later, set multiple points in place simultaneously, scattering them along the circumference in shotgun fashion. Once these anchors have been set in place, direct your attention to each point singly, moving speedily from one to the next.

But one step remains, to be executed abruptly, suddenly, and unexpectedly even to oneself: spread your attention along the entire circumference, speedily blending the preestablished points into a uniform band of awareness. Work with determination, quickly and decisively, as if you were to snap open an Oriental fan with a flick of your wrist, or were to sweep your hand across a bunched silk scarf, smoothing every wrinkle. On this basis the merged points will create an unbroken circumferential ring, at which moment, instantly, your expanded presence will fill the entire circle.

The two-legged form favors constancy and set routines. It combats shifts in awareness that jeopardize a person's sense of solidity. Interventions that could ease its burdens may instead stir alarm. Initially it will resist your efforts now that you have marshalled forces against its heaviness and density and the habitual routines of the mobile upright posture. Its counterattacks include hopping discontinuities—feelings of careening racehorse speed, or sudden moments of lassitude and inertia. Lulling itself in nap-like fashion, the two-legged form can impose the slow motion of everyday doldrums, deadening the quickness and efficiency needed for application of the method.

Above all, remain alert—guard your attention. You must cultivate alertness for any dismissive peremptory judgements that pass within the chatty dynamo of internal monologue: "Two places at once? This is mere fantasy, like daydreams or possibly madness. Come to your senses! Next you'll claim to have become a god." The remedy for such attacks is the rapid and precise application of the method. Therefore, hold dead-center steady and rotate dervish-like, projecting darts of attention toward the circumference of the encircling band of space. Relax into privileged moments of expansive freedom.

* * *

Abrupt cancelation of dreary burdens—no more partition of space![22] Physical configurations eliminated. Mental images all but nil. The landscape summed and solved.

Nighttime raids—touchpoints of flickering buoys. Our bodies—reliquaries along a pilgrim way.

Patterns appeared to your [inner] eye—pie-slice cuts of [radial] arrows, sweeping arcs terminating in space-pervading union.

And you, my dead-center watcher draped in star-flecked velvet—you were in-the-round and all-around. You became the eye of the circle when your expanded presence made you circumambient.

Gone, the insistent dragging along the body—gone, the daggers of our common plight—gone, the countless iterations of goodbye.[23]

And you, my flyweight teacher lolling in Klieg-lit pools of light—you made yourself into a little god before the two-legged form torched your wings, forcing your return.[24]

A MODERNIST MYSTICAL TEXT

Eye of the Circle is reminiscent of the laboratory scientist's logbook that holds reports of the day's experiments, procedures, and results. But mostly it is a training manual in which Teste's alienation from the everyday world is on full display. Valéry would like us to believe that Teste's method elicits an experience of expanded bodily presence. The body in question is not the physical organism, the two-legged form, but the lived body of subjective experience. Valéry was prudent to suppress *Eye of the Circle*, otherwise he would have betrayed his principle of coherent exposition in service of empirical truth. The extreme sensitivity illustrated in his piece, not to mention its mysticism, would have damaged his reputation as a public figure.

A telling point of comparison for Teste's circumambient presence is the divine attribute of omnipresence. As God pervades space, so Teste's practitioner is spread across space in an expansive ubiquity. In his fifteenth-century treatise, Nicholas of Cusa characterizes God as an infinite circle, its center everywhere, its circumference nowhere. He addresses God in phrases of which Teste's are reminiscent: "Your sight sees—roundabout and above and below—all things at once." His name for God—"true Unconstrained Sight"—anticipates Teste's circumambient field of awareness, the means whereby the practitioner becomes the eye of the circle.[25]

Valéry has written a modernist mystical text—mystical because Teste's method is designed to induce a transcendent experience, modernist because it abstains from traditional religious terms and symbols and shows no trace of institutional affiliation. It is the one instance of mystical writing in Valéry's otherwise atheistic body of work.[26]

Valéry eventually recoiled from *Eye of the Circle*, sickened and irritated. Consider the derogatory and dismissive tone of his proposed internal monologue: "Two places at once? This is mere fantasy, like daydreams or possibly madness. Come to your senses! Next you'll claim to have become a god." Consider the sarcasm of his final sentence: "And you, my flyweight teacher lolling in Klieg-lit pools of light—you made yourself into a little god before the two-legged form torched your wings, forcing your return." Valéry mocks Teste's hubris—"you made yourself into a little god." He indicts Teste's vanity—Klieg lights were fixtures of theatre and filmmaking and are easily recognized symbols of glamour, fame, and matinee idols. Finally, Valéry resorts to ridicule in calling Teste "my flyweight teacher."

Valéry's severity demonstrates the gravity of what was at stake. He had no real choice but to bury Teste's report in his *Cahiers*, otherwise he would have been forced to retreat from his self-appointed role as a man of science and rigorous thinking, of pure intellectual endeavor, a mathematician of verse. The publication of *Eye of the Circle*, even its dissemination among select readers, would have represented a calamitous retreat from the saving convictions he endorsed as a young man when he "resolved to think with rigor—to *not believe*—to consider as null and void everything that could not be brought to total precision."

Emilie Teste knew the truth about her husband all along: "So I said to our priest that my husband often reminded me of a mystic without God." The same can be said for Valéry, with *Eye of the Circle* the incriminating evidence.

Who is this character—Emilie's husband, Valéry's alter ego? What is his cultural setting? Teste is an anti-hero, the confident cousin of Beckett's Malloy. He is Apollinaire's confrère, absent a sense of humor. Teste is a mock-serious Dada-man, a habitué of Cabaret Voltaire. He is Tzara's shadow, his intellectual megaphone. Standing ramrod straight on the café's tiny stage, they chant reasonable absurdities about the mercantile potential of the Somme and the fiscal benefit of gas attacks. Teste is an acutely discriminating *flaneur*—a modified Faust without the prickly bearing imposed by lust. Eyelids at half-mast, he scans the tech gadgets and cake-icing artifacts displayed in the Parisian arcades, in the Apple Store, Costco, and Walmart, and in the insomniac's nightmare circus known as Amazon. Teste is the brilliant counterpart of Chaplin's Little Tramp, a trapeze artist juggling nitro-charged glassine packets. He is Josef K's *Doppelgänger*. He is a failed savior, a grade "F" bodhisattva: departing for his world of light, he casts a cold eye on the disasters that set the direction of our late-stage Kali Yuga. Teste is the swansong of the star-studded Enlightenment playlist. His tacit project, the project within his overt project, is sublunar rather than solar. He is the critique of instrumental intelligence, a homeopathic treatment for its poison. Corrosive in the extreme, he spoils the complacency allied with the mastery of technical reasoning. A zoomorphic analogy? Teste is a barnacled sea turtle—wizened, now a century old, he seeks riptides tending toward deep-water calm.

6. Oneiric Reports

Esoteric

Dear —,

You asked for a detailed description of my dream of the green snake. The original report was stored in your files, which means nothing now that you are paralyzed apart from your index finger—the finger with which you tap the keyboard. The dream remains vivid, as real as real life, only more so. We were amazed, we fell silent. An exchange of glances signaled our mutual awareness that the dream is a revelation. The green snake is a secret—knowledge of this kind is esoteric. I feel trepidation even now in fixing the imagery in writing. Do you recall the engraving of the alchemist who turns from his distilling apparatus and peers beyond the picture frame, at the person examining the engraving? He holds his finger to sealed lips in the traditional gesture signaling an insistence on secrecy:

> I walk slowly, stealthily, bent forward at the waist, to the top of a rounded hill and peer downward to the other side, where an enormous creature, a veritable monster, rests in a field of grass. Its body has many extended segments; or rather its body, which lacks a central axial structure, is composed of many extended segments. The grass is closely cropped, comparable to a putting green, and its color is an intensely saturated emerald green. The creature is tens of yards across and has multiple heads—one head at the outer end of each of its bodily segments. The overall shape of its tentacled body is a grid-like arrangement in which each of the internal quadrilateral figures is formed of opposing angles of about 50° and 130°, respectively. A black diamond-shaped pattern recurs over the entire surface of the snake's body; otherwise, the creature is bright green, the same highly saturated green as the emerald-colored grass. All the eyes of its many heads are wide open, permanently fixed in this position. There are no visible eyelids. The pupils, the sclera, and the external shape of the eyes look the same as human eyes, only much larger. The pupils are circular and black, as if fully dilated, and surrounded by a thin line of white sclera. This is a most uncanny and strange animal—vibrant, unique, an

awful presence. It inspires fear and fascination and is nothing less than numinous.

The creature is breathing, but not through its mouths, which remain shut throughout the dream. The entire surface of its body is a respiratory organ. A barely discernible rhythmic pulsation of respiration recurs throughout its skin, comparable to transpiration in plants. The creature subsists on air alone—it "feeds" on air. It does not eat food or excrete residue, nor does it move from place to place. It is not suspended, as if hovering, but rather it presses lightly on the ground, applying minimal pressure, virtually none at all. It is not subject to gravity in the way of physical objects. The creature exists in a supremely and uniquely balanced state, and its power is on par with its balance. It exists—simply that. It is alive, a perfected life form. I know all this for certain, precisely, in the moment.

The creature has not been placed here by an external agent, nor did it travel to reach this place. The whole matter of location needs to be turned around—the monster's creativity is in question. There is no place—no location—that exists anterior to this creature's occupying it. Here, where it presently rests, is a certain place because the creature occupies its present location. Other places are to be similarly interpreted. The snake and its place (wherever that place may be) cohere and form a whole, and it is the snake (rather than some location) that creates the basis of their mutual coherence.

I am fascinated and feel the danger of the moment, and the longer I linger the closer creeps the sense of incipient panic. I say nothing and move away as quietly as possible before awakening with the sense of having witnessed a secret of the highest order.

Now, touching finger to lips, I ask you not to share this letter or to publish my report in one of your books. Recognize the delicacy and power of esoteric knowledge: keep the alembic sealed shut. I continue to hope for personal coherence—of a scope and strength that will allow further investigation of this powerful vision.

Doppelgänger

Dear—,

You asked for a written report of my *Doppelgänger* dream—in fact, a double *Doppelgänger* in that two doubles are present. One is my true self, fully realized, the other is an odd cartoon-like rendition of my selfless body. Here is the report:

Across the room, standing fifteen feet away, is a man facing in my direction. He is solid, fully corporeal, and conveys a vivid sense of physical presence. Seeing him, I feel pleased and surprised to encounter a dear friend, and he appears to feel the same. Dressed in a tie and a tweed jacket, he is older and more heavyset set than me. I find him admirable and handsome. I retain my familiar physical dimensions and ordinary sense of self-embodiment—my body feels as it does in everyday life. The color of the room and its contents, including the man's clothing, is muted and dull, tending toward brownish gray. A small round table is positioned beside him, a few objects resting on its surface. He stands directly in front of a window draped with venetian blinds. The light passing through the blinds casts bars of light in the dimly lit room. His body blocks the sunlight—he is solid and opaque.

A strange human figure stands immediately to the man's right. Three feet tall and bent forward at the waist, he is pale and monochromatic and somewhat translucent. He moves constantly in the abrupt, juddering manner of cartoon characters in old movies. I have no interest or special feelings about this figure, and the man standing nearby appears not to notice him. The cartoon-like figure passes directly into the man's body with no apparent resistance, at which point it disappears entirely.

Now, once again, just the two of us are present. We attend closely to each other, eye-to-eye, intently studying each other's face. He is alert and eager, his expression is full of anticipation. I am struck with a sudden feeling of intense familiarity toward this man, and, simultaneously, I realize I am dreaming—I am the dreamer and the dream's main protagonist, both at once. I now concentrate with purpose, attending exclusively to the older man's face, and he likewise concentrates on my face, at which point I realize that we are identical, the very same person. At this moment, coincidentally, my double becomes highly animated—bright-eyed, delighted, smiling. Initially, I am amazed, then, moments later, I feel joy and gratitude paired with disbelief.

This is an impossible circumstance, I know it as such, and yet here we are, the two of us, both the same and different. Instantly upon recognizing the impossibility of this situation, I lose form and weightiness. My sense of embodiment evaporates, while my double becomes barely perceptible. The room has also changed: it has been reduced to a bare, vaguely sensed enclosure. I have become disembodied, utterly so, merely a point of conscious awareness that moves rapidly back and forth between our respective locations. The tracks of my movements materialize as fine white lines that crisscross the room, forming an insubstantial, ovoid, web-like pattern suspended in empty space. Suddenly, all movement ceases, and once again I am standing in my original location, fully embodied, and, as before, aware that I am dreaming these episodes. Meanwhile, the room is apparent but insubstantial. My double is present but lacks a sense of vitality and physical materiality.

The present outcome feels incomplete, like a disappointing failure. My plan is to muster utmost concentration and direct my attention at the double, in this manner forcing our convergence and making us identical. I recognize this plan as a risky, possibly dangerous endeavor with little chance of success. I begin nonetheless, setting my mind to the challenge. The alternating pattern of back-and-forth movement recurs, and, at the moment we merge, I awaken into full alertness, stunned with an intense feeling of emotional fulfillment.

This is a most subtle dream. I am reminded of the hall of mirrors at carnivals and fairs. Is the main protagonist not himself a double—a double of the dreamer? If so, four doubles are in play: first, the insubstantial double—more pencil sketch than a rounded character; second, the responsive, fully realized double wearing a tweed jacket; third, the protagonist, the main character of the dream, who executes plans and participates in rapid exchanges of interpersonal emotion; and fourth, the dreamer, who recognizes that *he* is the creator, the dreaming subject, when he awakens into lucidity. And yet no level of subtlety, no mirror trick, can capture the ease and gratification and sheer delight I felt upon awakening into perfect coherence with myself.[27]

Dreams Her Own Drowning

Sinking to the lake bottom, she dreams her own drowning. A seam opens, an abdominal tear, and from this parting of flesh come multicolored fish, singly, then in pairs and triplets. Vermilion, azure, phosphorescent green— lively forms arcing, darting, parading in jack-knife beauty through untwining coils of viscera veined in pink and maroon. The smallest fish casts sparks that inflame the foam bubbling on the surface. Other fish swim furiously, drawn to the light—flared gills and black lidless eyes set on the sparkling gem at the center of this rapidly evolving display. Wary and hungry they lurch and nibble its fins before tearing it apart. A prospect suited for dark-night imagination—a scene of speed and color enfolded in the undulating curls encircling the small fish and its attackers.

Not a Drop

I saw a pitch-black liquid penetrate the vertex of a perfectly shaped geo-metric cone filled to the top with a white substance. Not a drop overflowed. Black now substituted for white. It was destruction without dross. Fear chilled my spine.

He is as real as what he destroys, like carbon monoxide does oxy-gen, turning the suicide's complexion cherry pink. Consider the betrayal of believing a void is penetrated rather than a substance assimilated and destroyed. Naïveté and nescience hand-in-hand—twin children of evil.

A Single Mass of Perception

Dear —,

You asked for a written report of the unusual experience I described in our last session—what you called a hypnopompic hallucination and diagnosed as a parasomnia. I did prepare a report, but I see no sense in calling the experience a dream, normal or otherwise, much less a hallucination. I was awake at the time, alert and fully aware of my surroundings. I sat up and checked the clock. I scanned the room, attending to small details. Nothing was amiss, nothing felt strange. Diagnostic reasoning in the setting of a fathomless experience is trivial—like a water strider's suspended dance on the surface of a dark pond. Even now, months later, I yearn for the honeyed hues of that wonderful morning. Here is what happened:

> I passed instantly from dreamless sleep into the knowing center of absolute fulfillment. I awakened into a state of wholly encompassing, all-knowing awareness. The transition was instantaneous, as if a switch had been thrown. No lag, no grogginess. I knew in the moment that nothing of greater inclusiveness could possibly be known. I did not receive a new idea, or any number of ideas, even very abstract ideas. It was obvious in the moment that what I knew was ineffable. Nonetheless, I sought orientation, a verbal means of stamping the experience in memory, and a single word did come to mind: completeness, as in complete knowledge. Knowledge of what? Knowledge of all, all at once. Seconds passed in this manner. I surveyed my present state with a trace of detachment, then succumbed to intense feelings of joy and tranquility. I next began laughing, helpless to do otherwise. Emotion of this kind continued at comparable intensity for a few minutes. The entire day and the coming evening were burnished with a rich and gratifying undercurrent of emotional warmth. Seconds, minutes, hours—temporal markers introduce common sense but their meaning evaporates in the present setting. Throughout the day, I occupied the Now moment of a timeless present.

I have read your books—I know your training included studies in Asian religions. Do you think the *Upanishads* are merely ancient scriptures—quaint, interesting, dated? Why not break free of diagnostic categories and see that my experience corresponds exactly to direct knowledge of the atman, the lucent core of personality and the subjective aspect of the highest principle? Atman is called the *origin*, the *womb*. Another of its titles is the *Whole*, indicating completeness and the integral character of its composition. Participation in the atman makes one *the knower of all*. So knowing, one knows as does the atman, in a *single mass of perception*. So knowing, one participates in the atman's inherent qualities of *bliss* and *fulfillment*, recalling my feelings of joy, tranquility, and gratification. Were my experience simply a dream, a hallucination, a parasomnia, then everyday life is merely a fantasy of wakefulness.[28]

The Perfect Consumer

I dreamed of the perfect consumer—the king of appetites, a seductive and voracious character. I report what I saw:

He appeared to thrive on a superior level, exercising full possession of his powers. Tall, handsome like a matinee idol, and recognized immediately from his shredded chest and its heartless chamber.[29] *His trademark quetzal-feather headdress glowed in the colors of a jungle rainbow. Nearby, a crowd gathered in eddying coils, their eyes blinking and flashing like slot machines and retro neon.*

"Behold the man!" they shout, raising a chant that grows in volume. The crowd had met its master—a competitor who could kill them. A connoisseur of all things new and clever, he casts a cold eye on tip-top gadgets.[30] *An advocate of the average, he is the mime that compels crowd behavior.*

"Smart money!" he shouts. The crowd responds in kind: "Smart money!" they repeat, setting in motion their slave-singing shanty. Our man chortles and chants his heave-hoe sailor song, delighted by the formula's crowd-wielding seduction. He bites down hard and spits a pebbly stream of broken teeth. They lunge for the relics, fighting with their fists. Knives are drawn, gunfire erupts. Everyone is laughing—a birthday celebration for the king. "Our man! Our man!" they squawk, parroting one another. "He is a Midas of expensive trinkets—he serves us effluvia on tinfoil patens."

A dark moment erases his cheery countenance and taps a drum roll within his empty chamber—a lonely feeling as enticing as it is elusive. "Oh!" he moans in deep-deep yearning. "If only I could murder a shepherd! If only I could shatter skulls with my ox-bone cane!" He imagines serpentine glands, bloody and enormous. Their pulsing peristalsis settles his mind and calms his nerves.

Worrisome clouds suddenly part, his prospects brighten. His forehead wrinkles with cheerful menace. In the distance, he sees a shopping mall and parking lots that span half the horizon. Well above, dangling from the clouds, are ivy-shrouded pudenda speaking in foreign tongues.[31] *"How exotic!" he whispers. "I will tour there and take my friends." Like a cavalier Gulliver striding among the*

Lilliputians, he approaches the mall's main entrance where he grabs the glass doors' chrome handles and swings them open.

He finds the stale air bracing—breathing deeply, he detects six marketing scents, all personal favorites. The odor stirs his determination and inflames his imagination. "How wonderful! A dreamtime of needs and satisfactions!" Struck by a bolt of memory, he imagines the cozy glare of cut diamonds and the invitation of unwashed bodies. "All that's missing," he says, "is the chill of freshly moistened garments." His forehead is pinched, his lips pucker in bitter-lemon folds. "Now is the moment! Why wait longer?" Sternly whispering "Sieg Heil!" he steps across the threshold. The canned music spurs his gait, provoking a marionette display of confidence.

Alongside his crowd of friends, he rides an ark that rises on swells of vanity and moors at passing fantasies, while the world burns around them and ice melts into the sea. They relax in wooden deck chairs: feet elevated, martini glasses in hand, telescopic cigarette holders held at jaunty angles. They visit and laugh; alcohol has released their tongues and boosted their self-assurance. They believe the houses they see on shore are actually shrinking as their rudderless boat is drawn into the tidal furor of night. Their leader, our man the perfect consumer, stands upright in the cockpit, twisting the spoked wheel in erratic patterns.

Ruminant bleating suddenly pierces the air. Only a stone could ignore the resonant terror. Shortly the bleating becomes a snarling hissing rattle. The captain must be nearby, the pimp that runs the perfect consumer. I detect his wandering hands; I smell his gunpowder breath. Whistling a hypnotic tune, he sets the passengers adrift in a tide of firefly pleasures. A living form begins to brighten the darkness—curling and rising and becoming a smudge-stained aurora before condensing into a sawtooth crown hovering in the starless sky.

Put away the crosses, wipe away the tears. Rip the purple garment from the splintered stake that was once driven into the ground.[32] A wholly different time, last in line, has arrived. See the eddying bands, the throngs of disembodied faces drifting in beeping streams, led by a cheerleader decked in pom-poms, a sailor's cap, and the silk holster into which he inserts his phone.

7. Art in Due Season

The Pivot, the Hub

One bright afternoon, I walked along a downtown sidewalk, gritty concrete underfoot. Traffic to one side and buildings to the other, a bank squatting nearby. Plump cumulus clouds blotted the emptiness of the pale blue sky. Nearby oaks and aspens cast nodding patterns of spots of light. Murmuring engines signaled cars stirring a block away. This mobile urban scene encouraged close attention to the surrounding forms and colors and sounds. I stepped lightly until the unexpected moment when absolute silence poured into the moment, absorbing all the ambient sounds. So began a vision of seconds' duration:

> I am the pivot, the hub, the alert focus of a display of power reduced to simple geometric components. Insubstantial lines appear, like spider silk arcing across thin air and extending forward from the moving objects whose bristling energy yields motion. Adjusting spontaneously their length and duration, these intangible vectors of change thread a system of abstract signs signaling the direction and force of cars, trucks, and pedestrians. The physical composition of surrounding objects has changed as well. They feign solidity—their surfaces are suddenly erected, marginally durable means of holding in check the infinitesimal fury of tiny particles. The nearby concrete wall is brittle, a crumbly desiccated mass, as if encased in a superficial wrapper; so superficial I could thrust my hand to the wall's coarse interior without a scratch. Each object is a unique variant of packaged energy. A truck lumbers noiselessly forward. Beneath its hood is the metallic source of the crude, booming energy produced by the rhythmic explosions that pump its pistons. This crude means of locomotion is but one of many contributions to a wonderfully coherent display of lines and surfaces, all held in a vibrant balance of dynamic equilibrium that adjusts itself automatically and much faster than I can imagine. Power and movement are resolved perfectly in the play of lines and surfaces. Ordinary perception is muffled during this experience, its amplitude lowered, but it remains entirely accurate. I sustained two modes of perception; I lived in two worlds. It took advantage of me, and I submitted.

I sought a name for this experience, a title, that I might gain the advantage and pin it down. The first choice—*A Futurist Vision*—referred to the blustery Italian artists who formed the Futurist movement. They rejected the portrayal of naturalistically disposed space—for that matter, nature of most any kind. Above all, they valued motion, shiny machinery, the internal combustion engine, and the hubbub and commotion of urban life. Airplanes (in combining flight and machinery) were their angels. But the Futurists' stridency, their warmongering and adulation of violence, were naïve and ugly and made this title an unappealing label. Another choice—*The Transparency of Resolution*—recalls the advancing images of celluloid movie film. Light departs the projector and, passing through the film, creates a running series of forms and colors on the projection surface – an additive process analogous to a series of winks. Similarly, the urban scene of my experience was modified when viewed through a transparency of resolution constructed of visionary lines.

An artistic precedent that best captures the charged mobile character of the streetwise vision is Mondrian's concept of dynamic equilibrium. His late paintings accept flickering motion into his personal canon of acceptable content. The most active such painting (left unfinished at his death) is based on a busy urban street grid. The most superb of his paintings reflect a perfect merger of *ascesis* and aesthetics. In turning away from nature, he saw behind it, into hidden patterns of mobile coordinated unity. His own name for his work—*Nieuwe Beelding*—is best translated as *New Beholding* rather than the customary *Neo-Plasticism*. Mondrian's resolve to rely on primary colors and two-dimensional pictorial space was a sacrifice worth emulating. I recognized that a radical change in attitude was prerequisite to creating the paintings I desired, and Mondrian's were a vision of ethics arrayed in patterned coordinates.

A Peculiar Vacancy

Select a memory with evocative power, sufficiently vivid to bloom instantly in imagination, as when you glanced across the street and saw *the face*, unknown yet strangely kindred in spirit and eros. Summon the image, await its appearance. Say the name *sotto voce*, in the marginally audible whisper reserved for prayer and incantation. A change occurs, a door opens into a dimly lit room. Dulled focus numbs attention as feeling guides awareness along paths marked by associations equally diffuse and strong. She pulls away, the muffled sound of rubbing silk displaces viscera before lodging in your solar plexus. She turns, unveiling an oasis where instant springs saturate absorbent banks of heaped sand. Her eyes lock on yours—intense thirst held in taut suspension. Preceding these images and the poised uneasiness that set your body on edge was a moment of peculiar vacancy remote as a star, compact as the pulsing face of a rose. Preceding these moments of fixed attention was a chasm, ocean-deep and knife-edge wide, and a corresponding emotional charge set to gratify the yearning of urgent familiarity. My art inhabits this moment, this most minimal segment of time. Simultaneously quiescent and volatile, and set to expand like a nicked vacuum when the rushing absorption of surrounding air explodes its glassy surface.

The Overburdened Piece

No matter its technical finesse or formal complexity, the overburdened piece is mere entertainment, at best an amusing veil, an interesting shield. Better to see a wild animal pace the stage than watch a three-hour movie. Better to gaze on a cloudless azure sky than study the anvil-pounding shape of an expanding thunderhead. Venus astride the new moon is an interesting conjunction, but the nebulous bulk of the Milky Way is an enameled washtub full of blowzy wishes.

The successful painting must be clear and obvious. It must deflect curiosity and the search for meaning. There is nothing to its far side. Nothing is behind its mirrored designs, its geometry defined in silver, black, and gold. What secrets of execution it harbors are as invisible as its several layers of glass. No allowance is made for interpretation, and critical excursions are prohibited. But this is only half the story. Ineffability is a difficult subject for painting because it resists materialization. It fights against you like an enemy you feel compelled to embrace. It winks and nods, then leaves you flustered. Ineffability is the perfect disappearing act.[33]

But *something* must be painted, and its formal properties, its plainness and open-palm clarity, must have a mental counterpart. I have given this counterpart a name—*mirrored transparence*. Granted the work is successful, the person who meditates on the painting feels she is transparent to its ineffable subject.

Little can be said about a painting whose success depends on the exact coincidence of its formal and mental properties, neither of which provides signposts, associative clues that permit the eye to deviate from the painting's unresisting face. What one sees is the substantial presence of absence. Ineffability signals as plainly as a flag flapping in the wind. Is it a pleasure or is it a fearful prospect to have ineffability wink and nod, and appear palpably to one's senses? I would say it is a delight comparable to standing two inches from the Grand Canyon's rim.

I intend to become the painting—this is my goal, and once the painting is finished, I am what I desired when I first faced the reflected light of its mirrored geometry. The subjective outcome of this practice is detachment from the work of one's hands. The painting is now truly external, the bearer of superabundant objectivity. It assumes the status of an icon in a cult from which the artist is an apostate. One must make art to the end of surpassing the inspiration of its maker.

Spirit Catcher

Aerial prophylaxis—spirit catcher. Scarlet threads are strung wall to wall, floor to ceiling, forming a taut web across the corner of a brightly lit, porcelain-white room. Visitors huff and puff, their vanity chills the air. Collected after a month's suspension, the thread is boiled for tea. Sip slowly, savor the broth, drink what leaks from taboo regions of the imagination. This is a propitious negligee, but most of them will turn their heads.

The Cool of Late Evening

In the cool of late evening, I walk quiet streets until entering a dimly lit warehouse. Whispery drafts hollow the cavernous space. Shuffling footsteps echo from the galvanized metal walls. I puff and strain, positioning huge blocks of iron resting on castors until dozens of minute corrections create the desired effect. A vitrine positioned in the middle of this arrangement contains desiccated flowers discovered in a paleolithic grave. A chemical derivative disseminated throughout the building will reproduce the flowers' original bouquet: a tincture of sweetness laced with florid excess, an odor of unsettling intimacy cut through with the chilling rush of shadows bearing down like iron. The piece finished, I depart. Factory chimneys glow in the brassy morning light. The exhibition begins tonight.

Art in Due Season

DUCHAMP AND PLAY

I knew a lilt and spark upon stumbling half-aware on a fresh attitude toward the making of art. I would create temporary wholes of randomly dispersed pieces of junk. Nails, glue, paint—all means of adhesion would be avoided. The precarious temporal status of such work, always edging toward perishing, was appealing and desirable. Art would amount to temporary, beautifully coherent arrangements of discards and detritus. Surprise and spontaneity were counted as necessary marks of aesthetic discovery. Months might pass before a piece was completed despite its parts having been on hand for months, stored on shelves or littering the floor. Midwifery is a false analogy. There is no pain when the elements of the work spring into place. Caressed repeatedly by the maker's appreciative gaze, the whole would solicit its parts. The tegmentum of a successful work would be the instant certainty of aesthetic coherence.

Certainly, I was acquainted with Duchamp and his Readymade art. Duchamp was my sparkling saturnine guest. His project shared similarities with mine, but I meant to attack its indifference and cerebral finesse, its slap-in-the-face critique of Romantic conceptions of art. I had turned on his *Bicycle Wheel* and hefted his snow shovel. His upside-down urinal had exhausted its aura of historic importance—the piece was tedious, barely more than a tired cliché. I saw Molly Bloom atwitter, flat on her back, after tripping on the menacing coatrack Duchamp hammered to the floor. His funereal bottle dryer was hung with souls ripe for picking, like the identically shaped death-trees found worldwide in indigenous cultures. His bristling metal comb, his tumescent black typewriter cover, his shredded and glued string of shower caps hung wall to wall—all were so many moments of tedium spent contemplating eros and dust. His Parisian apartment door, made to order, told the whole story: it was simultaneously open and shut.[34] I knew the revolutionary bearing of each piece, its role in his artistic development. But I found in Duchamp and his Readymades too narrow a band of experience, too constricted a heart, too parched and ironic an intellect.

One goal was to step past Duchamp and let the door he opened explode from its jambs. The resulting passage would restore aesthetic forms and feeling to foremost importance and situate them on a new level of mental engagement. Successful artwork crystallizes moments of intense aesthetic focus that target physical objects, simply locking the aesthetic into its material counterpart. The resulting artwork is a physical object, freestanding, independent of its maker. An artwork is not theatre or performance and does not substitute for political strategy. Nor is it simply conceptual, shorn of matter, save for lines or letters or some other explanatory message that have been printed or scrawled on the wall. Aesthetic consciousness is necessarily a materialized reality; in practice, an ongoing embodiment of subtle, quick movements of pure concentration. An artwork must be tangible, its material conformation must be three- or four-dimensional. Materializing an aesthetic remained a goal. Duchamp taught as much despite abdicating (temporarily) the role of the artist as a creator of objects. My point is confirmed by his posthumous barn door, the peephole of which reveals a cool voyeuristic scene of intense eros. The scene's sylvan setting is simply a reversion to tradition—a pastoral installation with an overt, free-wheeling erotic text.[35]

The strategy of creating tangible works that captured moments of aesthetic intuition required the accumulation of the discarded material that was later used in composing new pieces. I needed an eye for junk that promised complicity in our common effort to transcend the mundane. I hunted aimlessly for parts that heralded unknown wholes, and these parts were often remnants of previously completed artworks that had been disassembled after exhausting the span of their emotional half-life. The discovery of parts later used in completed pieces was accidental. By definition, all such discoveries must be accidental—a matter of stumbling upon shards and fragments and, quite often, a thoroughly anonymous part which by merit of wear, sun, or age gave no sign of its previous purpose or identity. I considered serendipity a subsidiary expression of creativity.

My home was a dreary hovel during these experiments, its contents more esoteric but less colorful than Schwitters's *Merzbau*. Upon entering the front door, one confronted a cherry-red caned chair suspended from the ceiling with transparent fishing line. A coil of inch-thick jute rope rested in its seat, one loop dangling down, nearly touching the floor. The disturbed expression of visitors suggested a subtle *auto-da-fé*. Relief arrived when they turned to the mantle and saw a small Mongol shaman: his robe woven of sun-bleached denim, his upraised arms made of crescent okra husks, his head taken from a Japanese Kabuki puppet. Works like these were disassembled once their vitality was depleted. No piece was allowed an afterlife of stale or dead meaning. None was photographed. Their parts were stored and reused when imagination dictated a rearrangement of the sensations and feelings cued when the original pieces were created.

The personal experience of creativity was signaled by a sudden about-face, a gentle but startling call to attention when an isolated part enraptured the heart, withheld signs of purpose or meaning, and blocked mnemonic associations. Creativity was an instant crystallization occurring in a null zone where structures of beauty and meaning jumped into focus like a falcon striking its prey. The discovery of parts—the parts later subsumed into a whole—was an odd moment imbued with affection: eros absent touch, love without defilement, a personal contact shorn of ulterior motives, especially the motive of saving the part for its eventual consummation in the final work. A prime source of artistic failure was to seek a part specifically for the purpose of later assembling a whole: to act purposefully in an effort to construct an artwork as useless and purposeless as were its parts.

Purposely creating artwork by means of purposeless methods posed the risk of falling prey to analysis and idle talk. No mental trick would work here. Recognizing the irony of purposefully applying purposeless methods complicated the moment, clouded the mind, and spelled the demise of creativity. Redoubling the bifurcated Cartesian mentality—"Oh, but now I have become aware of the awareness of the irony!"—created an additional burden of obscurity. Detached awareness of the situation was an intrusive interference that deadened creative vitality and tore limb-from-limb the coherence of self and part, part and whole. The wordy awareness of an unengaged yet observant intellect spelled a chilly transcendence remote from my revitalized junk. The risk at hand required jumping free at first notice of the problem and doing so suddenly, quickly, efficiently, with maximum foresight and subtlety.

The solution was to jump free and remain clear of the entire theoretical muddle. Time and again I was benumbed by love and dazed by laughter, gales passing like breeze stirring aspen leaves. I wanted to turn art into an occasion, not a purposeful production based on the intention of representing something useless. I made friends of things and trusted these friendships to bring others a delight similar to the delight these things had given me. Little can be said about art of this kind. It evades the wordy intellect and occupies a null zone untouched by critical thinking.

Cursory examination of a finished piece might yield nothing when the accompanying biographical details are withheld or ignored. The vignette of a piece's creation added personal nuance and served as a bond uniting the artist and the person to whom the piece was given. This was important for pieces born of faceless play because their lightness of spirit tended to disguise their high seriousness. The vulnerable shyness of such pieces might hide an adamantine gem. The trick was to see the gem and recognize its exact material expression in the work at hand.

Listen to the story of a common tool's transformation into an unearthly implement—a masculine tool neutered by sudden awareness of its complete uselessness. This is the story of how the artist's late-summer discovery of a certain tool made him empty, free, and happy. The dust kicked from his feet settled quickly. Its fine granular texture matched the heat and dryness of the air. Nearby mesquite trees were poised and ready to shed their cicada-shaped pods. Doves passed overhead, their wings huffing a barely audible whisper. The looming manor house, empty and deteriorating, rested like a dry-docked galleon on a patch of drought-struck earth that had never been plowed or paved. As he walked on the brittle grass of the balding skull of cracked soil, his eyes settled on a pair of partially buried pliers—old, pitted pliers of rusted iron dropped accidentally from a working hand. He reached down, eager to fortify the stock of tools gleaned elsewhere on the abandoned estate, and what he felt was warm sandy dirt before realizing his fingers had gone numb from holding not an ordinary pair of two-armed pliers, but the single curved arm of a pair that had long since fallen apart. This numbness flowered in a silvery place cool as breeze, fresh as roses. Now he held a fish, a dolphin, a set of enfolded dovetail curves—a most piscine of abstract forms bearing a circular eye. Now he held nothing and felt it to be just that—he held nothing in his hand. His gratitude mounted, there was no word to describe the freedom. Impenetrable tranquility unmapped by language and fenced from words. As evaporated moisture forms clouds that fall as rain, so laughter showered the moment and made personal and close what is inherently empty and selfless.

The work was brought to completion when the half-pliers was plated with sterling silver. The piece was called *Thulé*, a diminutive of *tool* and the placename of a location in mythical geography far to the north, tempered by constant spring weather. *Thulé* was given a friend, who recognized, immediately upon grasping the plier, its embodiment of such mixed properties as silver and iron, beauty and corrosion, comfortable heft and the lightness of punning good humor.

≈

The high seriousness of art put to rest, play became important. This was a low seriousness, a playfulness of lowly origins. I found discarded materials appealing and susceptible to aesthetic discovery. Superlative finds promoted amnesia of their origins, either ugly or urbane. Trinkets scattered on the grounds of a neighboring tenement were the detritus of poverty and museum-worthy displays. The barns and sheds and the abandoned greenhouse, the goose pen's silent hissing, were so many prepped fields awaiting the sowing effect of imagination. Red seeds dispensed from the sweet Southern belles of magnolia blossoms were bled from the land by a hundred years of family residence. Material surfaces scored by decades of abrasion held my attention, as did the lathe work of slow growth on the bark and heart of trees. It hardly mattered whether the shapes and lines that drew my attention were bulky as a stump or compact as the red clay hardened around the sharp angles of a certain quartz crystal. But I did have a distinct preference for the small and the diminutive, for dimensions that misled one to expect little when great shifts of scale and the feeling of bigness were right at hand. Some discoveries were accompanied by ghostly presences. Hephaestus stepped from the shadows of the shop and stood beside the workbench before dissolving into a smithery array of affections that reassembled themselves as the old man who pointed in the direction of my little wooden chair left partially repaired three decades before.

Moistness enhances the beauty of agates found washed ashore. Time dries their surface and does the same to one's initial keenness. So it was with the discoveries that served art-making during this period. The great leveler—the talons and black-lace mantilla of passing time—could blunt a work's initial intensity and smudge its meaning. But when the parts of a previously finished piece were tended in the bright aviary of imagination, they retained a certain freshness and readiness preparatory to their ingathering in a new whole.

The gathering of parts into a newly composed whole was sometimes imbued with ritualistic features. Consider my transformation of a wooden trellis, fire-engine red and shaped like an abstract tree flat along the dimensions of length and height. Each limb of this "tree" projects outward from the central trunk at a 90° angle and runs parallel with its neighboring limbs, the whole series like the symmetrical skeleton of an equilateral triangle mounted upright on its base. This barren tree, ablaze with angular intensity, conveyed an ominous threat. I asked: The dress of which season sets this tree in such apparel? It was the tree of an intense fall—a fall that sought to arrest the violence and barrenness of the human estate. Come the days after Palm Sunday, as the Passion deepened, the trellis was draped with black gauze. Situated to the side of this arrangement was a lovely figure of Lalique glass, a nude posed identically as the mermaid in Copenhagen's harbor. Her turned head allowed a sidelong glance toward the draped tree. Directly above her head, suspended on a red thread, was a bleached deer tooth, and circling this tooth was an actual bumblebee frozen in mid-flight. All brides should be so intent on their lover rising for a second coming, as if from the dead.

SHIVA AND THE THINKING WAND

Not all the religiously toned work created during this period was Christian in form or content. Consider my lingam-and-yoni, a variant of the symbolic coupling found throughout the Himalayas and Indian subcontinent, in areas noted for Tantra and devotion to Shiva, the dancing phallic destroyer. The lingam was a black porcelain insulator, a medium of bolts of electrical power. It rested upright in a sterling silver bowl tarnished with a dark patina—erect, glassy, a rising force passing within the silver lips of the circular container. The lingam-and-yoni was encircled with a black mesh made of heavy-gauge wire. This was menacing, sharp-edged fencing, a protective measure equally brutal as the object it protects. The coupling embodied a tectonic force, like rising thunder breaching a dark sky, paired with the recognition of the sky's need of earthly support. Apart from its sense of constrained violence, this piece was a failure. It was more nearly a thunderbolt pure and simple, rather than a symbol of the balanced complementarity of earth-and-sky. Kali was too much involved and, consequently, the lingam-and-yoni was too dark to signal a perfect match. The piece was too chthonic a symbol. It did not represent a fair exchange; the partners were not of equal rank.

Christians tend their religious symbols, and should a symbol die for lack of congruence with the worshipper's soul, they nurse it back to life through moral obedience, fearful guilt, and clerical models of subservience. This is cheap religiosity, common sanctimonious fare. Pagans, in contrast, do *puja*. Because the gods live not once but always in their religious implements, the possibility of worship remains ready at hand, and the call to obedience is driven from within the object, not layered over a skein of empty symbols. Liturgy does not require a secret abacus handled by priests: it is instead driven forward when the object itself directs the heart in ritual behavior. Religious implements, having become the habitation of gods, must be handled with precision.

Puja is not a Sunday chore. Set the religious implement on the shelf—the god is present but untamed. Some gods are unruly houseguests; few are friendly shepherds. Even those who tend cheerful domesticated humans can become dangerous in their lax behavior or florid displays of emotion. The uproar of drums, timbrels, and reedy wind instruments can unsettle the air. The tidy domestic calm is disrupted when anxiety is stirred by the wrong placement of religious objects. The space near adjoining walls becomes palpable when the god's mood invisibly thickens the air. The room's occupant is susceptible to disturbed attention and worrisome thoughts when passing through the dense atmosphere of the god's favorite corner. If the god is feminine or a flowery masculine presence swarming with perfumed nymphets, then the dour face of the room's little scholar may succumb to clenched-jaw frustration over so much sanctified eros. Let the god slip beneath a recognizable degree of personification and rejoin the earth from which it emerged, then the trouble at home only deepens. Then one does *puja*, not to enliven a textbook picture or to revive a dying god—one is compelled to act for the sake of emotional survival. Pleasing the god has become a serious matter rather than a Sunday chore.

All this was learned through art, and it was a matter of bondage and chagrin to find an artwork compelling action by forcing its own liturgy. The piety of the lingam-and-yoni included the placement of flowers at its base. Marigolds were appropriate, a faded iris was fitting. The piece was shrouded as needed or moved from one to another location to conform with the ambient light or the seasonal moods of the earth. Finally, this piece was biased rather than rounded and complete. Its aesthetic was dumb, its symmetry was plain, its emotional color was too close to black, and its earthiness made it overly heavy. The piece was disassembled and its parts not used again. Its power routed tranquility and playfulness. Even after disassembly, its vitality continued as a visual image with emotional repercussions. This is all to say it captured deep-seated verities of imagination. Because it was isomorphic with the corresponding archetypes, deeply rooted in collective imagination, the piece permitted neither the liberty of play nor the play of liberated aesthetic consciousness. In certain respects, the piece was a success, and for the same reason it was a failure. Aesthetics differs from mysticism.

Setting the lingam-and-yoni in repose did not dissipate Shiva's frenzy. Simply disassembling the work did not dispose of the corresponding imaginal image. Its dark form had been etched in my mind. A more effective balancing act was needed, a means of off-setting Shiva, such that everyday life might resume its usual stability. The risk otherwise was absorption in the force field of his black sun, reminiscent of the erratic tilts of a little car blown about by passing trucks on a windy highway. To this end, I purchased a flat-black metal sculpture of *Shiva Nataraja*, only five inches tall. This classic example of sacred sculpture is a compendium of religious symbols. His braided hair, arched and flying; the lunar crescent woven among the braids; his right foot pressed down, squashing the squealing demon. One of Shiva's several arms points to his upraised left foot. The cupped palm of another hand holds the fire of cosmic conflagration, which flares outright when another of his hands pounds the circling drumbeat of creation-and-dissolution. These are grand gestures with purported metaphysical significance, but none has the ascetic importance of the *mudra* of another of his right hands. This particular hand is positioned in the *abhayamudra*, the gesture of fearlessness: his open palm, signifying liberation from his own dancing round, is directed outward toward the supplicant. Shiva himself provides the panacea for the discontent he creates.

A small gold ball was attached to Shiva's braids, and four silver rings were set in place on his flaming circular corona, marking off quadrants. The point was to balance and personalize his wild display, bringing the god within the compass of ordinary affairs and assigning his attributes to domains of experience with which I was personally familiar. Shiva, unbridled, is unruly and divine and chaotic. Tamed Shiva, though remaining a god, is more nearly familiar. The gold ball was the decorative end of a post earring given to me by a psychotic patient.[36] Making the earring the god's bauble showed that madness is his adornment, his destructive play. That the ball was gold and spherical told of the ore of understanding that might be found in the greed of madness. Rounded and overripe, the god's madness is like the snake's skin shed for the sake of revolution and renovation.

Other artwork during this period that captured spiritual concerns did so only through allusions. Overt religiosity was curtailed or erased; aesthetics was given due centrality. I had come to see that artwork must not be bullied by the impersonal concerns, the blunt emotion and the fundamentalist tendencies of religious preoccupation. Greater freedom was needed. Consider my little stupa, an upturned cloisonné bowl whose interior displayed turquoise-green leaves and rosy-white lotuses set against a blue ground. The bowl's base was now its top, and this new top functioned as the platform where a white wooden spindle was attached. Using the spindle as a handle, one could turn the bowl upside-down and gaze into its azure-blue hemispheric hollow. The piece was simple in form, as simple as it was pleasing to the eye. A simple gesture revealed its concave loveliness. The wispy lotuses and typical cloisonné colors alerted the astute viewer to its being a diminutive version of true stupas, a traditional architectural expression of Asian wisdom. In this manner, the piece played with scale—the small beckoning the very large.

Another piece from this period focused on Krishna's epiphanic visitation at the State Fair of Texas, a crowded regional celebration held annually in Dallas. This was a matted and framed collage in which two images appear as different aspects of one and the same photograph. One image is a postcard showing the figure of Big Tex: the gargantuan, lore-bound, papier-mâché cowboy that looms over the central courtyard of the fairground. Tex is dressed in blue jeans and a red shirt. His cowboy boots are big as a house, and his yards-wide belt buckle shows a longhorn skull in bas-relief. His right arm is braced against his chest. His left arm, swept upward to his side, welcomes visitors. Tex's hundred-gallon cowboy hat sits like a roof above the frozen smile where his mechanical mouth drones on and on: "Welcome to the State Fair of Texas!" Such is Tex(as), a towering cliché of gassy braggadocio. The other image of the collage is a vividly colorful, surreally detailed drawing of the youthful Krishna dancing on a beast whose body has nearly disappeared under the mass of writhing snakes that form its head. The two images, carefully interwoven, portray a striking scene: looming above the fairground courtyard, his face a weird toothy grin, is Big Tex, who surveys dozens of fairgoers stepping blithely around the mass of snakes, which, thanks to Krishna's foresight and power, are kept within the bounds of peaceful cohabitation with the blasé humans. The title of this piece escapes me, but I do recall my confusion in the crowd and the gratitude I felt for Krishna's actual followers, whose timbrelled chanting was the day's peaceful leaven.

Playful and yet decidedly esoteric, another piece warned of the dangers of religious preoccupation. This was an old brass thermometer made of a circular dial mounted on an octagonal base. The arrow indicating temperature was steely blue, sharp at one end, a flared crescent at the other. An advertisement had been printed across the thermometer's face:

REMEMBER
THE NAVARRO COUNTY ABSTRACT CO.

Immediately beneath the advertisement is my addition, cut from the text of a magazine:

So it is seldom that we have
extended verbal reports from

All this meant nothing apart from a firm command to remember something rare and abstract, sensitive to heat and cold, and related in some obscure phonetic manner to a Texas county whose name recalls an Iberian province where a certain master of post-Reformation mystical abstraction made his home. I assumed (wrongly) that John of the Cross passed his childhood in Navarre. Indeed, two volumes of his work sat on my shelf next to the thermometer. The language of this piece turned colloquial and agrammatic and suggestively randy when the thermometer was turned over, front to back. Cut-up script scissored from the same sentence that appeared on the front of the thermometer had been pasted on its back:

t hed om
ai no fecstatic
to me.

Shuffle these letters, closing certain spaces and opening others, and set them at the end of the phrase on the thermometer's face:

so it is seldom that we have
extended verbal reports from
the domain of ecstatic time.

The interested viewer was next inclined to reexamine the passage on the back of the thermometer, recalling that the humming sound of *Om* is viewed as the sonic equivalent of divine omnipresence in certain Asian religions:

> To heed Om ain't no fecstatic to me.

So it was in those days. Mystical abstraction and ecstatic emotion posed worrisome risks, but a good fecstatic could effectively turn the mind from these grandiose concerns. Now was the time for preparing extended verbal reports of past ecstasies, not for the continued pursuit of such experience. The thermometer served as a warning and a source of humor and self-critique. The preliminary sketches and bits of cut-up sentences that contributed to this piece's construction were stored in an envelope marked with the title *Thermomenotes*.

In creating sculpture, I considered handiness a virtue, and portability a natural consequence of handiness. I also saw that the adequately handy and portable piece is necessarily simple. These qualities, which formed a coherent set of aesthetic criteria, were means of counteracting conceptual complexity and overly subtle allusions with the promise of something tangible and easily wielded—something enjoyed simply on the basis of its physical presence. One work that met these criteria was made of a deer antler in which the brow tine has been substituted with a red wooden spindle. The relative dimensions of the parts of this hybrid object conformed perfectly in the way of a successful surreal combination, but without the jarring or bizarre effect of Lautréamont's rendezvous of an umbrella and a sewing machine on a surgical table. The antler elicited touch: it called for manual examination, and yet its rounded shapes and the mutual suitability of its parts caused the hand to grasp gently or else to refrain altogether from touching. The piece rested oddly and solidity on flat surfaces, tines downward, the tip ends of most tines touching the table. It was simultaneously hunched and luxuriating, and lacked the weightiness one expects from bone and wood. The person to whom I gave this piece immediately tested its handiness (its conformity with one's palm and fingers, its ease of movement when handled) and took pleasure in its abundant uselessness.[37]

Prepared for travel, another portable sculpture was a darkly stained wooden box coated with high-gloss varnish. A clasp latch was attached to one side; a brass handle had been nailed on the top. The box, which contained the parts of an assemblage, was quite narrow, two feet in length, and swung cleanly at one's side. Its contents were to be displayed on the floor: a green camouflage tarp was laid down like a tablecloth, and several pieces of dark iron were arranged on its surface—the largest a crescent-shaped arc resembling a scythe. Despite the dreary colors and the piecemeal and ominous tone of the piece, it was not dull. It was an infernal machine, both martial and comic. It recalled Tinguely's self-destroying sculptures and a Rube Goldberg tutored in Hades. The downcast, mock-humbling gesture of walking in circles around the piece while looking downward appealed to me, as did the compactness and handiness of the piece when packed for travel. It was entitled *Picnic*.

Another portable sculpture, called *Thinking Wand and Carrying Case*, captured an entirely different tone than *Picnic*. Rather than drawing attention downward, it lightened its bearer through an emotional antigravitation effect. The Wand was a sun-bleached wooden stick worn smooth from the redundant abrasion of ocean waves. Affixed to one end was a black oval disc with white bristles at its base and a corona of colorful fibers radiating from its circumference. The Carrying Case was a white ring strung with smaller, vividly colored rings, which rattled and spun freely as gesture dictated. The rings, bristles and fibers, and the black disc, were made of sun-blasted plastic. Each was a bit of trash washed ashore and scavenged on a Gulf of Mexico beach. The piece was constructed spontaneously, on the spot, and its creation coincided with my discerning its purpose. The Carrying Case transported ideas, colorful rings of thought. The Wand functioned like a reverse lightning rod—rather than modulate bolts of power for safety's sake, it blunted and dispersed thought and released the mind from seriousness. The Wand was an erratic antenna designed to create static and foul clear pictures, in this manner preparing its bearer for the vision of a coastal sky as blue, blustery, and bright as a Dufy seascape. The piece was an instant success. The Carrying Case was grasped in one hand, elbow bent as if hefting a suitcase, and the Wand was held upright alongside one's head. Decked in this fashion, I ran along the beach, skirting the surf, sea breeze swelling my sails with gales of laughter.

CROWN OF THORNS

A spirited art of play and aesthetic intuition was not born overnight. Its conception coincided with a disabling wish for personal transformation: its gestation overlapped the disintegration of my personal life: its birth was an extended affair of the heart marked with delicate tensions and the sequential leaps of freedom that attend early romance and the birth of a first child: and its development included trysts with several styles of art that had thrived for decades. These styles were courted with seriousness and a sense of finality; thus, each step forward was a leave-taking equally exciting and sad. I set about assimilating the precedents of contemporary art by means of study and practice. Dada and Surrealism stirred interest, less so Impressionism. Dullness inhibited my appreciation of Cézanne, though I recognized his importance as a bridge to Cubism. I found Picasso dull and heroic, and superabundant like a pregnant cat with a dozen wombs. Early Cubist collages were wonderful, but Analytical Cubism struck me as a misnomer or possibly a farce. There was not a system or an analytical program here but random variation punctuated with formulaic personal habits. The chill and brownish tedium of some of these works can serve as a pictorial analogy of the disarray of an era over which the angel of Hiroshima reigned. Braque's late paintings of his studio are a whole different matter—in my view, the greatest Cubist works painted. Their interwoven, flickeringly illuminated translucent planes hover well above the Cubist norm, like a stunningly layered sky overarching the crawling autos below.

Abstract Expressionism stirred a personal reaction of emotional upheaval. It hardly mattered that my opinion and feelings about the movement were dated even then. Extremes of scale interested me, and these were painters who liked BIG. That the act of painting might engage whole-body gestures was another point of interest. Barnett Newman's panoramic color fields sliced with vertical "zips" seemed as big as the rice grain I once saw in a museum, its surface covered with an entire sutra written in microscopic script. My admiration was encouraged by the fact that Newman dabbled in Kabbalah and that Reinhardt, an educated man, wrote radical theory. I thought of Rothko, Reinhardt, and Newman as saintly heroes. I made a pilgrimage to the Rothko sanctuary in Houston—a fetid moldy setting for his umbers, reds, and roses, but a fitting site for Newman's sculpture of a pyramid surmounted with an inverted obelisk, which to this day sits rusting in its reflecting pool, succumbing to the ugly urbanity of a petroleum-financed purgatory. Despite my adulation I thought of these painters as distantly situated meteors, of less consequence than the hyper-gravitational fields established by Klee, Mondrian, and Kandinsky.

It was clear to me that I had been Paul Klee during his mysterious sojourn in Rome as a young man.[38] The oddity was not that Klee was dead while I was alive, but that Klee and I had merged for only the first two years of the twentieth century. Our strange relationship was based on a discontinuously sequenced metempsychosis in which the soulful overlap of the two persons does not correspond with the lives of the affected bodies. I do not believe Klee died in 1940, when he is supposed to have died. More than two decades later, to the indoor side of a frost-rimmed second-floor window, I saw him painting at a small easel while smoking a little bent-stem meerschaum pipe. Were Klee dead, I too would be dead—but I am alive, therefore Klee must also be alive.

Klee's adult life merely extended his Roman sojourn, drawing it into an increasingly enriched mirage of fantasy. Examine his travel diaries, watch the stolid Swiss evaporate in the sun of Mephistophelean intelligence. A pellucid dawn becomes a vaporous pall as the sun turns away, its burning face replaced with a massive black sphere whose rippling fracture lines recapitulate the course of modern painting. Meanwhile, a feathery array of jeweled fragments float toward the sea floor where alternating moments of fission and fusion disperse and magnetize the sparkling shards. There, seated on the ocean floor, notepad in hand, rests the demigod imagination of Paul Klee. Who is this magician painter—an insect, an elephant, a god or a mite? He is all people to each thing, and each thing to the incipient person from which we each spring.

My identity and Mondrian's were isomorphic—a closer relationship than mine with Klee. As Mondrian's Theosophical studies provided an esoteric rationale for his theory of Neo-Plasticism, my similarly inclined, alchemically tinctured thinking served as a theoretical buttress for the purifying exercise of the mirrored glass paintings I completed before the ultimate stage of a playful aesthetics.[39] I studied his work: the color tones, the stubby light-touch brushwork, the sculptural effect of canvases raised slightly, in stairstep fashion, forward of the frame, and the crinkles and hair-thin cracks of aged white paint. I emulated and basked in the tranquility of Mondrian's mastery of aesthetic balance. I executed a series of paintings that both incorporated and challenged his stated aims.[40] I dwelled on the rare photographs of his Paris studio. His whitewashed walls and Spartan surroundings might have been identical to mine—were it not for my balking at Mondrian's final touch of painting a flower white and letting it stand as the sole remnant of the natural world.

I thought of Kandinsky as an alien of superabundant skill and talent. My skies were dull compared to his cerulean Russian nights. His colors, utterly sensuous: to have carried this degree of delight past the border of realism was a titan's feat. Studying one of his circular, highly fluid and elaborate canvases in the Philadelphia Museum of Art, my head rotated 180° from the upright posture, I saw perfect balance, omni-symmetry. Kandinsky lived an otherworldly artistic perfection. His doing so without becoming eccentric and strange seemed the mark of strategically modulated inspiration. Nevertheless, he did falter. Certain pinks and roses in later paintings and particularly the extraneous curlicues are failures. Wizardly colorists can fall into enthusiasm when the decorative leanings of interior design spark an irresistible seduction.

Immersion in the traditions of modern art set me straight in several respects. Indeed, *straight* is the word. The formal properties of painting held my attention: more so line than color, especially straight lines. Symmetry became a personal dogma, granted the symmetrical counterpart to a visible feature might be invisibly lodged in the viewer's mind. All parts must be set precisely, and the whole composition must settle into resolution and possibly tranquility. I was a purist, too much so, until I determined that the concepts that inform a work are miserly substitutes for actual material configurations of intrinsic beauty. I tested the perspectives of Conceptual Art and Earth Art and found they adulterated my effort to make material works that adhered to tradition while simultaneously surpassing it.[41] The old must be retained to the extent of sharpening and silhouetting the new. There remains room for play within traditional constraints. Abandoning all traces of tradition is like a one-shot episode of dropping the mic: interesting for a moment, possibly stunning, but boring thereafter. Its typical outcomes are dreary flat-footed instances of self-absorption.

The frame must be preserved and the picture set on the wall. Loyalty to a picture's fantasy depth is a meaningful bridge to tradition, even when that depth has been reduced to the millimeters-thick surface of brushed paint. A surprising light may surface from within a picture and overcome the passivity of its flat surface. What might then happen is a reversal of the usual subjugation of the picture's figure to the viewer's gaze. Consider my self-portrait matted in dusky pink and framed with unstained pine. Not a realistic portrait but a page from Vesalius's 1543 anatomical text displaying his exquisite engraving of an unhappy skeleton. Its right arm is propped on the spade that dug the open grave at its boneyard feet. The left arm is lowered, palm open in supplication. The skeleton's jaw juts forward, its eye sockets are hollow and dark, and its tilted skull gazes upward. A desert landscape recedes toward the empty horizon, echoing the futility of the skeleton's barren Jobean call. Inviting visitors to have a closer look, I would take the picture from the wall and position it against a window or another source of light, at which point the skeleton would pair-up, in exact recto-verso fashion, with another of Vesalius's engravings, in this instance a nude woman (whole, not dissected) exhibiting the canon of proportion. The two images were fully and simultaneously in view, and symmetrically disposed. The skeleton's left arm is perfectly counterbalanced by the nude's similarly angled right arm. The mirror play is striking, even boggling, when intellect is brought to bear as an aid to imagination. Light/dark, left/right, recto/verso, male/female, dead/alive—permutations of a single pluripotent theme. The resolution of these antinomies was simpler than words and found expression in the sighs and smiles elicited when I held the portrait to the light.

Romance is a barely viable subject for late modernist art. The risk of sentimentality is never in full retreat, and the lyrical expectations of work concerned with romance were anathema to a skeletal rhetorician of symmetry. Nevertheless, romance prompted the creation of two pieces from this period. The one entitled *Hylas and the Water Nymphs* is a horizontal collage framed in dark triple-beveled wood. Immediately beneath the glass is a brown paper sack, wrinkled and punctured with fire-scorched holes. To the far side of the holes is a delicately colored painting of Hylas stooping to fill clay jars, meanwhile nude water nymphs surface among nearby lily pads.[42] Hylas was sent to fetch water after Jason and his shipmates anchored in Mysia. Poor fellow was no Odysseus, and he had no wax to plug his ears. His resistance dissolved in a flash: the nymphs dragged him under. He was helpless before the liquefying enticements of mercurial shape-shifting beauty. So it was with the kohl-rimmed eyes of a nymph of my acquaintance, her burn equivalent to mine.

A later sculpture I particularly liked is *Boxing Glove*. This was a multiple—a series of ten identical keychains produced at my instruction by Ringside, a company that manufactures and sells boxing paraphernalia. The bauble attached to one end of each silver chain is a clenched, perfectly shaped miniature boxing glove made of black leather with red stitching, the word "Ringside" woven into its cuff. Printed in scarlet red, in Times typeface, across the glove's dorsal surface are the words

DEUS EX MACHINA

Originally a theatrical plot device, the God-from-Machinery effect was also a theological stratagem of the Deist movement. The artwork represents a blast of physical force channeled in punch-like fashion, to the end of resolving an intractable dilemma that demands either victory or defeat. Such is boxing, and such is the fully embodied life—the life we eventually come to know as dragging along the body. I gave a keychain to a quadriplegic friend, formerly a mentor, whose sole means of voluntary action was movement of his right index finger. He attached the keyring to the joystick he used to manipulate his computer, his sole means of communication. The meaning of the DEUS EX MACHINA boxing glove, he wrote, is "maximum ego effort." I understood and appreciated the heroic potential he discerned, but my personal interpretation was quite different. My interpretation circled our inevitable victimization by the physical body rather than our marshalling power over fate. The piece captures, in the simple way of clearly executed profundity, the outcome of our lives of dragging along the body, day by day, until the end. An unseen punch, perhaps a left hook cartwheeling across one's blind spot, puts full stop to the game. In the body's machinery, God hides the blow.

~

Certain principles figured prominently in the artwork of this period, reinforcing one another and constellating a general attitude. Their personal influence was gravitational and compressive: they drew feeling and focused attention. One such principle was impermanence. Museum walls had begun collapsing in 1960s, and the stable face of my world had been eroded by Buddhist studies. I rejected the belief that artwork should be permanent and protected from the rigors to which other kinds of objects are subjected. In consequence I sank more deeply into a cool vat of anxious freedom. Exacerbating the unease of coming freedom was the principle of self-abnegation. Were I to grasp freedom, I understood that it would not be *mine* but the possession of the nobody to which my name was attached. This was a troublesome prospect. I inhabited a personal world porous to the worlds of other persons. Could my world and the others be lived artistically? Can nobody exist without the supports of name and habit? I assumed so, insofar as life was punctuated sufficiently often with Joycean epiphanies and Proustian privileged moments, with Surrealist revelations and the lapses of consensual validation that call forth the willing suspension of disbelief.

Surely so, I thought, as long as purity of intent was the watchword of artistic creativity. Purity of intent—my harsh master and ready doorman.

Purified intent focused traditional aesthetic criteria on materials that have been found useless or ugly. It set upon the fluid axes of the field of consciousness the discarded rags and bones of a bloated, irreverent era. The outcome of this sensibility was a series of works combining highbrow intellect and lowbrow materials. Couplings of this nature took form under the influence of sudden intuitions that functioned as disclosures of religious truth. To the perennial philosophy of mysticism was added an artistic avant-garde. My art became more than me, and my role in this equation was to vanish like a cloud diffusing across an empty sky. In my place, at these moments, was spirit, which can be imagined as a cat transfixed by a mouse—poised, precise, ecstatic.

Play and gesture coincided as my art reached its most elevated expression. *Play* is understood well enough by analogy with the activity of children. Its deep background touches on the dreamy philosophy of Maya and the three Moirai, the spinning sisters of Greek myth whose hands weave the textures of fate. *Gesture* is less easily grasped despite the stunning simplicity of actions that pass as true gestures. Gesture is unlike a handshake, a friendly wave, a courteous smile, or the arm's movement while brushing one's teeth. It is more closely akin to a shout or a yawn or a sneeze, or to scratching an itch or stumbling. Gesture is a skeleton whistling in strong wind, a speeding martin in flight, a fire that thrives after all its fuel has burned. Gesture, raised to its highest power, is the transparent embodiment of purified intent—and when this intent is aesthetic, then, in the moment, one's life becomes an object of art. This is not a wishful fantasy, and it is wholly unlike the dandy's vanity. Rather than life mimicking art, life is incorporated as art. Gesture is spiritual life in the raw.

Gesture and forethought are mutually contradictory, as are gesture and reasoned reflection. Gesture dawns outside the mind—its home is not within the cranium. The world provides the implements of play, and gesture sets them in motion, at which point thoughts, feelings, and presences both real and imaginary are fused in broadly encompassing states of awareness. These unusual and valuable moments are characterized by the infusion of artistic intent from beyond the boundaries of the ordinary mind. Gesture dawns outside the cranium; conceptual forms neither capture nor compel it. But this does not mean a gesture is ineffable, only that its material operations (as when a work is conceived and made) do not obey and tote the barge of logic. So it was that myth entered my art in due season. Not myths as told in books, but myths discovered in gestural action. Things told stories and encouraged engagement, and disseminated the stock of memories they held in common with humans both present and primordial. Artistic gesture opened the door to myth without the hinges giving the slightest creak of aridity or reification. I was taught by things without pedantic intent. I was bound in sweet freedom to things set free from dictatorial intellect and the pragmatic constraints of instrumental intelligence.

Consider the deft burial of an ax bit in the flat top of a squared cedar post. One swift blow divided the post perfectly along its vertical axis, and the instant of that division passed in an incomparable swooshing sound as fibers parted like a tree before a serrated edge of lightning, like darkness before a child's flashlight, like seawater before the arm of a god, like a broken heart before the beloved, like meaning itself when one squares off, face-to-face with the first dead body. The parting of wood, particularly the swooshing sound, not to mention the resulting cedar aroma (same as ancient coffins), opened the golden, unmarred inner surface of a tree. Then, springing forth, a presence whose faintness matched its allure. Then came understanding of why an early gnostic intoxicated with divine immanence put these words in the mouth of the incarnate god:

> Split a piece of wood: I am there.
> Lift a stone, and you will find me there.[43]

A single swift blow of the ax set in motion a timeless gesture sustained for minutes. The work made itself—I was simply a privileged attendant compelled to weave a circle of thorns made from the vines of a nearby bush, to affix it onto the bare face of the post, and to suspend in the middle of this thorny crown a brightly colored parrot feather—blue, yellow, red, green. Art of this kind, in which direct action is forged of gesture and purity of intent, begs to be given away, otherwise it dies, and does so quickly. Insufficient sacrifice of personal attachment further mars its transience. The cedar post was set on the mantle and later passed to a friend, and with its passing I, too, passed. Art is a happy grief.[44]

8. Artists

Lumbering Gait (Marcel Duchamp, 1920)

Other men breed chickens and cattle or tend to bleating sheep. I breed dust woven with stray hairs and particles of desiccated mouse droppings. Hardly more than spindrift, like the spider webs that traverse the transom window. What I breed is the material residue of passing time, increments of invisible change. The dust swims in streams of pallid light before settling on a sheet of plate glass three meters tall and resting across two sawhorses. The project seems as trivial as a weakly wheeze. My work is evolving toward complete obscurity. According to plan, Man's photographs are recording its development.[45]

Apart from the bed and chair and the chipped white stool, my apartment four floors above the street contains a glued necklace of scissored bathing caps suspended beneath the ceiling.[46] The monochromatic honking of passing cars rises from the street. The variable pulse of traffic signals the time of day. What machines we have now! But none as perfect as the wooden propeller Brancusi and I saw eight years ago at the Aviation Show.[47] When I was a boy, machinery had yet to dominate life. People rode in horse carriages. Cars were rickety and unreliable. The machinery of our elders' lives was delicate and poorly assembled, all but pasted together. The men took pride in tailored suits. Pride was the lifeblood of that detestable lot, my father among them. The women dressed for funeral rounds no matter the day and marched their *petit pas* to the new arcades. The men, mincing along beside them, walked like tightly bound bundles of sticks. Their shops and arcades were baroque confections of spun sugar, their attractions sickeningly sweet. All those people traded in sentimentality, the cheapest armor of eros. The men loved to shop, same as the women—acquisition was their game. But my life is different. I harvest ideas with a merciless scythe and strip things of their absurd social accretions.

Paris in those days was quite something. Roché and I pulled up a few skirts. I miss my antic accomplice, the loyal friend who called me Totor.[48] We drank and caroused and rested for weeks between outings. The traditional artists kept to themselves and their special clubs. The Surrealists I met flirted with madness and shadowed flea markets instead of museums. They invited me to join them, which was simply impossible. Their pope was a long-winded angel, a littérateur with a repulsive pompadour. He carried his nose like a gondola sports its *ferro*. His imagination was as turbid and mossy as a venetian lagoon. It was his prose that was beautiful in its mimicry of the falling curve of a breast and the rocking spandrels of hips in motion. His search for Nadja was a romance fit for the new comic books. *Amour fou!* —how cute.[49] The Surrealists claimed to have mounted a rebellion, which I understood perfectly. The strangeness of their work evolved toward cliché; its prettiness gave it away. Dada was their baba, but I get by without extraneous fathers.

Kurt Schwitters knew the trick of chance combinations and the flirty chaos of destruction. He was a magician of beauty, an original—the later Surrealists were classifiable. But I have no interest in creating another *Merzbau*—a *merdre haus* that would make my life salable. The Surrealists smoothed the edges of their destructiveness—not one of their sculptures would draw blood. I refuse to seduce the eye. I felt something corrosive, a taste for chaos, like grit in the eye. I had no redeeming *things*, no *art* to offer as an alternative. I could no more join their club than forget the nub of destruction that seems never to go away.

Motes of dust vent upward in airy drafts. The bone-dry sash windows occasionally rattle. A bare lightbulb dangling nine inches from the ceiling casts a rotating ovoid shadow. I am greatly tested. Is it that I can see only gray, or that what I see is truly gray? A fragment of Heraclites is to my liking: "it is death for a soul to become moist." Drought is my method, my way; there is no end of the salt I seek. I snuck in Heraclites when the professors praised Descartes. This was before I, too, became Cartesian, my best disguise yet. They say reason guarantees objectivity—another of their wishful fantasies. Are the bones revealed in the new X-rays more objective than the strangeness of peering inside a human body? My game has worked well to this point. A rich heiress buys my work—I can pay for food and rent. I dine on pasta with a pat of butter and drink a single glass of red wine.[50]

The past few years I have dreamed three times of an African desert where lustrous elephants traverse dunes and salt pans, their massive feet gingerly transporting the vast bulk of their bodies to the sea. I feel the soft drumbeat of their momentous gait and forward passage as they move through platinum moonlight. The lumbering elegance of weight distributed in perfectly coordinated patterns stirs my heart. I am greatly tested, now more than ever. Is my gray life forever drought-struck, or will I reach the blue waves and the penumbra of light that spreads across the white sand beach. At times I feel I have already arrived, where open palms wave boats to shore and flowers nod in idle splendor, before awakening to honking cars, the rattle, my throat dry as a desert.

Blue Smoke of Tobacco (Paul Klee, 1939)

We arrived in Berne the week before. It was Fall, days before my return to a boarding school on the shore of Lake Geneva, near Charlie Chaplin's house. A twelve-year-old, I was granted the privilege of wandering the streets. The rationale for my freedom was twofold. A mannerly, handsomely attired American boy, I could be trusted to return to the hotel at the appointed hour. I had walked the streets in Khartoum, Nairobi, and Rome—Berne's were far safer. Meanwhile, my mother could enjoy uninterrupted time with the man who would soon become my stepfather. She was svelte, elegant, and blond. He was warm and hearty, and the metal cleats affixed to the heels of his mountain boots were particularly impressive. My worry was the enforced quarantine of our pets after their trans-Atlantic flight to our new home in Switzerland.

I reached the Aare by way of a steep, rocky path that descended directly from the Bellevue Palace. I crossed the river's swirling eddies on a footbridge and began walking the cobblestone streets of Old Town. It was evening, the sunlight blunt and dim. Bricks, mortar, and stone, and bent chimney pipes pouring smoke. Footfalls echoed in the distance. Yellow light illuminated apartment windows. This was sixty years ago. Central Berne felt medieval.

One café remained open, its only customer hunched over a sketch pad, drawing with a pencil stub. His blocky forehead resembled sculpted wood. His widely spaced eyes were set beneath steeply arched eyebrows, his face fixed in an expression of surprise and anticipation. His complexion resembled old parchment warmed to the point of curling. Apart from his eyes, he looked ancient. He appeared to enjoy handling the little pencil and pretended it stubbornly resisted his manipulation. He would cup the pencil in his right hand, then stiffen his forearm and rotate his torso to adjust and readjust the pencil's angle, as if he were feigning paralysis in this mighty struggle. He then shifted his posture and, working with his left hand, pecked a number of dots and scratched several more lines. A figure took form on the pad: gaping eyes and squared torso, and outspread arms surrounded with dry scratchy strokes. It was fixedly contemplating, big-eyed and staring, its wings spread wide as if it had been violently blown backward into a position of high tension, as if a storm prevented the angel from closing its wings. I could read the man's lips when he raised his eyes and whispered *Angelus*.

After finishing his coffee he packed his things, slipped into an over-coat that fell well below his knees, and departed the café. I followed at a distance, unobserved. He paused twice—in the first instance he bent and inspected a small object on the sidewalk, in the second he touched the ma-sonry face of the building at his side. Intensely curious, nothing escaped his gaze. Two minutes after he stepped inside a doorway, light poured from a second-floor window. It was the same man, and behind him a woman wearing a vividly colored kimono moved about the room. He sat down in a straight chair positioned in front of a window overlooking the street. Two matches flared in succession, then another, at which point blue smoke rose from his small, bent-stem meerschaum pipe and curled around his head. It was dark now. He peered outside and looked exactly where I stood, nearby a streetlamp at the corner. He raised his index finger, held it upright, then circled an invisible spot in the air. I waved in reply and he responded, puff-ing two concentric rings of smoke.

Ten years later I discovered the work of Paul Klee. I read about his scleroderma, a painful skin condition, and studied a photograph of his drawing *Angelus Novus*. I am certain it was Klee I followed from the café that evening in Berne. But I cannot square this certainty with another fact: Klee died seventeen years before he signaled me from his second-floor apartment window.

Fast-Running Equilibrium
(Piet Mondrian, 1941)

I arrange space in perfect patterns. Equilibrium is mine after twenty years of struggle. I work in four dimensions, only two of which are actually seen. Now, late in life, I have turned to motion. There is nothing you might recognize—trees, sunsets, streams, unless you see that red, yellow, and blue are metaphysical, far more than optical effects.

The gallery shows bored me after I arrived in Paris. Their renditions of common things were exercises in tedium. Several artists had begun painting hayfields and watery tapestries and the promenade grounds of the bourgeoisie, and in this fashion they illustrate their *impressions*. Light on water is fine enough, but a pointillist science of colored dots is a poor excuse for lack of meaning. I sought and discovered something wholly different. I transform life in my paintings—fulcrums that lift the entire weight of aesthetic culture. I have succeeded time and again in painting a fast-running equilibrium that registers in sighs and momentary cessations of respiration, followed by the distinct feeling of an exquisitely peaceful balance.

I could improve their lot were I to paint automobiles or their war machines, and I might even stir some kindness if I painted the beggar woman near the kiosk I pass each morning. But my work stops at the easel. I am not a public man. Others will carry my inspiration into the streets. I am ill-suited for the fight, too thin and old, too crane-like in my isolation. My days of signaling sudden appearances of beauty have nearly finished. A coming danger is the cheapening of the spirit. I see its approach, mere decades from now: equilibrium reduced to decoration, ugly renditions of the costly need that moves my hand. Fake sighs for sale, and alligator handbags with sterling clips shaped like a Brancusi. Is beauty exposed in the market the same as beauty reserved for solitude? The nudie shows in Times Square sell beauty in bleached overexposure.

It is quiet here as cities go. The hum of traffic is not unpleasant. I occasionally hear airplanes, clattering beasts passing in midair. They say anyone with money will soon be able to fly across the ocean. I hardly care.

Tonight, Sylvia and I will dance a jagged foxtrot. Thelonious will visit the basement venue. His fingers are like wooden clubs—how does he manage such precision? His entranced shuffling, a woozy march across the stage in bedroom slippers, is too wonderful to bear. His syncopated rhythms track the pictorial music of my own Boogie Woogie.[51] I laugh when imagining the club. Sylvia says I dance like a stork or a spindly heron, like a happy egret hoofing the midnight beats. I have no doubt Sylvia is a bird, at times she is an exploding covey. Her genteel neck surpasses description—lovelier than Léger's cylinders and more calming in its fleeting moments of torsion than any of Boccioni's.[52] Others turn and look when we step on the dance floor. I ease forward, then suddenly reverse direction. I turn and shift and feign falling over, and when I bend sharply at the waist my suit lapels arch like the wings of a descending flicker.[53] Sylvia wears her silk dress black as night—its luxe applique of blue and green tulips flares at galvanizing angles. I huff and puff, all for laughs, but Sylvia is a bottomless well of beauty.

I love the Negroes' laughter. How they manage such elegance traces to hidden wellsprings of beauty. They treat me as a friend, perhaps because they recognize me as another estranged pilgrim. The white faces arriving from downtown are like tea-stained porcelain, reminders of what I have overcome. All things pallid are my enemy, first of all their paper-thin morality. The white faces sip gin poured from silver flasks. They mostly watch, and when they dance, I am reminded of Italian puppetry. I know this type; their daring is fueled by fear and liquor. Intoxication shapes their faces into masks of irony and sophistication. They cannot love, they think church occurs on Sunday. They do not understand that eros can strike from above. The Negroes, who are better informed, know it comes full circle: high-to-low, low-to-high, bearing the same meaning as a sphere revolving on its axis.

At dawn the white faces are ferried in taxis to gray buildings where sleepy doormen in livery greet them by name. They ascend by elevator. Brass doorknobs snap shut minutes before they sink into feathery beds. Meanwhile I will have retired to my easel, eager to catch the morning light. I position colors on two palettes, one reserved for pure primaries, as sunlight crests through the high windows. Real intoxication is fast-running equilibrium, a distillate of perfection. Even now I quicken the race in a final redemptive flight, testing my talent against music and noisy streets. The colored tape the Americans invented speeds my progress.

I learned persistence from my father, a craftsman before commerce forced him to become a shopkeeper. He was Deco in his wood carvings of abstract forms. Customers lost interest. They wanted impressive dining tables and chests as big around as their torsos. They wanted surrogate bosoms suited to their insipid taste. My father built a chair that appeared to levitate centimeters above the floor, and a table whose tapering legs ended in pinpricks. A confused shopper felt compelled to set crockery on the table—he said the extra weight was needed to keep the table from rising to the ceiling. My father and I are alike, we struggle against the materiality of real things. My mother was a cheery beacon of optimism and delight and dedicated to her craftsman husband. Both were sad when it became necessary to open the shop. Neither lived long enough to see that I have captured equilibrium. I miss them terribly, I wish I could show them my recent work. She would smile and laugh. "O mijn God!" He would say. "My boy, now you've done it!"

Paris was not a bad place, not until the frightening end. The city bustled with artists. My group published a journal, only two issues because the plates were so expensive. Three weeks were needed to turn my apartment into a studio. I hired a worker with a tall ladder to clean the clerestory windows. Colored panels hanging floor to ceiling created the proper volumetric balance. All the rest was painted flat white, including the table on the landing and the vase holding a single flower. A woman friend said it felt artificial. Of course! What the eye sees is inevitably artificial.

There were frequent shows, new openings most every month, but dark currents were already present. I could feel them in the street, like the changes in barometric pressure that signal a coming storm. A group seeking the surreal seemed to know war was coming. Their leader was a surly prophet. Marcel avoided their closeted mysteries. He favored chess over café life and was hardly seen in public. He and his one friend were carousers. I once spotted him a block away—the disciplined ease of his unhurried gait was unmistakable. I called out, "Can you play chess with blocks of space?" I won't forget his delightful answer: "Only in four dimensions."

My group fell apart soon after I arrived in Paris. I disagreed with van Doesberg and his ally van der Leck. Windmills, dikes, and foggy lowland marshes were too deeply embedded in their memory. They were cornered in their resistance. They sought flatness, the merely two-dimensional. They stalled for lack of sufficient abstraction and the fear born of constant departures. They painted for present times—I paint forward into the future. I suppose I have already departed, only Sylvia and dancing make me doubt it. My premonition of war proved true to life. History is an angel blown backward, shrapnel wounds dotting its lovely face.[54] The war will pass but not the tide of cheapness.

Fast-running equilibrium . . . I seek it each night in the dark of night and dream of it after the world of daytime images has fallen asleep.

9. After the Water Receded

Ominous Signals, Deathly Quiet

I will speak without codes or sleight of hand and tell what I saw after the water receded.

I crossed the mighty river on a buckled bridge, burned and curved like a singed ribbon. It was late afternoon, the sunlight at steep angles. Pearly clouds floated on oily silted water. Beside the turnstiles at the entry gate, I saw a boy's body hoisted on a flagpole, his dangling pants flapping in gusty wind. Nearby, a girl had been propped on a metal bench, her expression fixed in a horrible grin. I heard strenuous whispers and avid buzzing before seeing flies emerge from her mouth and ears and cluster on her eyelids. A man wearing a tailored suit had been killed by flying debris. His left temple was bruised red and yellow and badly swollen. Papers spilling from his smashed briefcase danced along the street in hopscotch fashion. Ricks of broken furniture and heaps of rubbish burst into flames against the foreshortened horizon of the urban scene. The fire curved in serpentine fashion like the stylized waves in Japanese woodblock prints.

The pylons that once supported electric lines had collapsed into coils and crumpled mounds resembling the clenched forelegs of a giant praying mantis. Electric lines lay across puddled rainwater, acrid and sizzling. Beads of lighting flared over pools of water, arcing between neighboring puddles. Apart from the sizzling and crackling, it was still and quiet. Insects were thriving, mostly beetles. Meandering scarabs pulsed like tiny cesium torches—they had found their natural home, a coprophagic heaven. Never before had I seen cockroaches crawl in a leisurely fashion. It was too early for the rats.

Strange-gaited animals milled beside nearby buildings. Every few steps they skipped and executed an awkward hop. They neither barked nor growled, but squeaked, a sound comparable to bats' echolocation pulses. Their sloped hyena-like haunches were paired with scoliosis of the lumbar spine. The oldest of these miserable creatures could do little more than run in circles. Scientists who predicted such changes have been surprised at the speed of their arrival.

I walked into the silicon heart of the city, the pivot that kept the wheel turning. I heard a tinny cacophony of whispers and screams emitted from cellular phones heaped four feet high at major inter-sections. Such were the panicked, plangent voices of the preceding era. The temperature gauges affixed to lampposts had exploded—the streets were crawling with skittering runs of mercury. Blasted lim-ousines, parked at skewed angles, resembled monstrous centipedes frozen at attention.

Apart from the boy, the girl, and the businessman, I had not seen another human. The surviving workers had been transferred to other sites soon after the water receded. I could smell the diesel fumes of their departing coaches. They say a workforce may yet be needed, if only to dispose of debris. Blinded decades earlier, and mute as fleshy robots, the workers passively submitted to men wearing suits with sharply tapered trousers.

I walked through claustrophobic neighborhoods inhabited by immigrants a century earlier. Bricks and mortar, wood rather than metal. New money had displaced the former residents, thousands of them over decades, their hearts' intent come to nothing. An art gal-lery stood empty and bare like a parading ingénue—naked, white, and elegant. Any lingering avant-garde had been ingested decades before, suctioned down the gullet of commerce. The newspapers dis-played on kiosk racks were devoid of print. Bylines had long since become meaningless, and yet the market for hard copy had never died. Two bits bought empty pages, wordless silence, a few moments of meditative rest.

I glanced upward upon hearing the huffing sounds of crowded wings in flight. Overhead, moving more deeply into the city, I saw a sky-spanning murder of crows. The dry complaints of their in-flight observations were like joking, dark-humored conversation. I followed them around a corner and came to a cemetery created soon after the city was founded. Its wrought iron was blasted and twisted. Birds by the hundreds perched on the gate and fence and the branches of trees. Other birds traipsed in dinosaur fashion around a bier made of a heaped mound of vines and lilies. A girl with a porcelain-doll complexion and wearing a sky-blue dress had been laid on the flowers. Alive or dead, I couldn't say. This was a scene of mesmerizing sepulcher beauty, as haunting and mysterious as crawling orchids. What I then saw, plain as day, was her apotheosis: she rose, simply levitating, her body punched through with bars of light colored in an orderly sequence of spectral patterns. She next dissolved entirely, all within seconds. Any sense of corporeal solidity gave way when she was transformed into a blue vapor that hovered momentarily before disappearing.

The birds suddenly took flight, lifting upward like rolling thunder muffled in cotton batting. It was then I heard the keening and the glottal ululation of one of the newly formed bands of mourning—the straggling, knotted lines of singers that had begun crisscrossing the land. Women, men, children of different ages—our future in the soft hands of persons capable of discerning the true scope of suffering. The children were mostly on foot, the younger ones were carried. The adults were dressed in rags and singed smocks. Runaway workers wore the sanctioned uniforms called Happy Suits. Trailing figures, all but ghosts, wore tunics, and when they paused at odd intervals, all motion ceasing, the closest resemblance was a Hellenic frieze. Later I realized the strangest element of the entire scene: none of the roving band was weeping. They had passed into tearless lamentation.

I left the park and walked deeper into the city. I became lost before discovering I had returned in circumambulatory fashion to its silicon heart, the pivot that kept the wheel turning. It was here, barely visible above the debris, the overturned café tables and the heaps of shattered mirrors, that I saw the upraised lance, a white pennant tied beneath its arrowed tip. Of all contradictions, the mounted pennant rose to the level of supreme paradox. It whipped and snapped in gusty wind. The sound sharpened my mind and enlisted an absurd sense of confidence. Following at a distance, I never caught a clear view, only heard soft chatter reminiscent of cooing doves and whispering children. A swooping, thrumming sound, like moths milling beside your ear, echoed off the buildings. Its volume soon increased, meanwhile the voices joined in a chorus that seemed to come from all directions before focusing on me.

Further passage is blocked when I stumble at the rim of an excavation site that extends as far as the eye can see. Another world is now in view, where leaden skies weigh on pock-marked plains and the lapsing strata of a tortuous stratigraphy recede into darkening shadows. Distant mesas blink in marvels of razor-sharp lightning strikes. A watery luminescence colors the glowering sky in the lurid green and wet-velvet blue of a mausoleum in Ravenna. Scattered brush fires flicker across distant plains, humming like approaching waves of cicadas. Nearby, I see crevices opening and magma rising, and great heaps of flammable gadgets, an ear glued to each one. Buffeting gusts blow from opposite directions, raising columns of grit. Legs, arms, and tasseled viscera pass through the air like shoals of fish. I see iron café tables, perhaps a dozen, stacked with coins softening and warping in the heat—the money is melting.

Bulging tubas pulse in erratic beats. The buzz of punched tambourines sizzles within burlesque tunes pumped from battered

*accordions. Shuffling crowds gasp and cry, plunge and fall, strangled
and coiled, ivy growing from every orifice. Men with dollar signs tattooed on their foreheads are dancing naked, impervious to the heat,
puffing humid clouds of breath-mint sweetness. Spooked children
twist hurdy-gurdy cranks. Women clutching headless babies shout in
peacock voices while circling mounds of daffodils bleached in halo-
gen light. In my nose, the scent, the odor, the smell of a carrion race.*

*Hordes of two-dimensional forms advance in cartoon fashion,
prancing with loose-limbed hipness. The ground beneath their feet
momentarily becomes transparent. Farther down I see eroded human bodies standing chest-deep in a slurry of ice. Blue sparks of
burning acetylene flash across its surface. Their mouths are black
apertures round as circles. I hear wheezy cries and awful moans sustained for seconds. I start to weep, reasonable despair having broken
loose from its internal mooring. I feel dizzy, my legs give way. Peering
downward, I cry aloud, "Will it ever end?"*

*Backtracking had become impossible. Compasses now behave
like a whirligig beetle—ticking here, spinning there, and reversing
direction for no apparent reason. It must be true, what I heard: the
earth's magnetic field has frayed. Continents changed shape like
spilled water as the ice melted into the sea. Fixed tectonic coordinates have vanished, only maps remain: patterns of empty signifiers,
invitations to sentimental journeys, none rooted, all grounded in
times past.*

*We could have known, evidence was at hand, strange events
were reported years ago. Rural folk said mountains spoke on moonless nights. Solar flares were observed with the naked eye in broad
daylight when the dimming afternoon sun loomed just beyond the
horizon. The Northern Lights were seen nightly for two weeks from
the Rio Grande River, near Laredo, then later from the equator before winking out entirely. The Southern Lights adopted recognizable
configurations—a horned pig, an octopus with eyes at its arm tips,
a hornet with human ears and a Cheshire Cat grin, a slick black
lemur with green eyes and canine teeth than extended far below the
jawline. Children worldwide gathered for impromptu recitation of
the dead languages they received in dreams. Important men had
begun to recite nursery rhymes during business meetings—a mis-
calculation doctors attributed to a rare form of epilepsy. It mattered
to hardly anyone that years had passed since birds were last heard
singing.*

*All true navigation was now based on dead reckoning. The
acoustic Doppler of travelers' screams substituted for radar and GPS.
I walked for hours, stumbling over broken asphalt, and screamed*

140

at regular intervals, listening intently before locating the buckled bridge. My fatigue was nearly unsurmountable. I remembered our race of women-gobbling titans whose power led to the present chaos. It was beyond reason to think the earth might once again assume a steady course.

My horror has dissipated since departing the city, but my fear continues unabated. More powerful yet is the grief that heaves through my body. But even this is preferable to the ominous sense of foreboding that seeps from the earth beneath my feet.

Waves of the Glorious Splendor
(Isaac of Nineveh, 7th c.)

My intentions are unblemished, pure as Nineveh's cathedral bell.[55] I will labor on high and ride the waves of the glorious splendor to my home beyond the highest heaven. I will avoid invention and vain thoughts and the ease that depletes the vigor of practice. Vigilance informs every waking moment and shields me during dreams.[56] I lie beside the sleeping man who bears my face and worries. I listen for his breath, his whistling gasps. I anticipate his turning before he rotates on the mat. What he dreams is clear to my inner eye: the market whirl, tapestries and silk, the rattle of coins, beads, and bracelets. He is the sleeping man, the man I see asleep. I am his keeper, his shield and protector, the rhythm of his chanting, his balm and the sweet odor of his tallow candle. I am his shepherd, he is my sheep. I am his cupped fingers blocking the sun when bad nights become stumbling mornings. I walk beside him to the well as he struggles with his thoughts. I take his arm and guide him. I am his holy double, the life he is unable to lead while awake. I am the father of my own self. Pray, Father, help me help my son.

They made me a bishop when I most wanted silence. My ill-spent act of charity was exhausted in three years when I moved from the palace to a stone cell built on a mesa above rock-strewn ravines. The well is a distance away. I peer over the desert at sunrise and see a pair of cupped hands protecting my eyes. Visitors bring oil for cooking and the lamp. Onions, radishes, lentils, knobby little potatoes. The men usually come in groups, the women usually come alone. Women who visit twice ask what I do here. The men are troubled by my stability—I am rooted here, in dust and stones. Restlessness is their state of being. They remain homeless, no matter their location. It is impossible for them to understand that I am continually rushing to meet what truly matters. They come when they have been crushed by failure. Their pride masks their feelings of futility. All are grown, some are warriors, but they differ little from boys who resist compassion with feats of courage. A few of the younger visitors have understood our life, but they must burn like warhorses before they are ready to join the brothers and sisters in the desert.

What I do is labor—mostly at night. Practice was once grinding toil, now it is easier and often pleasant. My palms, forehead, and knees are callused from prostrations. My knees wobble like an old mule's. I can no longer see at far distances and must hold the heavy manuscripts close to my face. They say I will soon become blind. The warmth recurs occasionally, my entire robe wet with perspiration. Feeling accompanies the sweating. I have difficulty remaining in my body.

I know my cell and have memorized its surroundings, each stone along the path to the well. The water jug lasts two days, then I take my stumbling walk to the well four stadia away. Sighted or blind, it hardly matters—I am always upright, standing continuously in the glorious splendor. I am racing into a future that already embraces me. Each moment, day by day, I feel wonder in the face of novelty.

Many of the brothers are advanced in love and would shed their lives for stillness.[57] They come to me, an older brother, and call me Father. A man twenty years in the desert said: "I tell you in very truth that if I go out to pass water, I am shaken from my habit of mind and its order, and I am hindered from my work and from the accomplishment of my rule of prayer." His intent is virtuous, his method extreme. True, even urination can be made into a practice—a means of examining the bulk and outline of organs within the material body. Not one experience is empty. Every event is an eddy in a passing current, a reminder of what we leave behind.[58]

I no longer wrestle with wandering thoughts—they return of their own accord. I recite the first few lines of vigil readings and for the rest, if I stand three days, I stand in awestruck wonder and feel no weariness at all. I am near the goal, I feel sure, and yet it recedes as I approach it. Will it end, can it end, this pursuit that binds every sinew? In another world, were I deprived of a body, I might ask for it to continue forever.

The merchants were coarse men who talked about camel trains and desert tracks, and the caravansaries stretching inland from Antioch, Aleppo, and Edessa. I was taken to their meetings where we sipped smoky tea from Chinese cups and lounged in upstairs rooms covered floor to ceiling with beautiful carpets. They would have cast me out if I had mentioned my own Father, who years before took me by the shoulders and said, "We are both now in the Spirit. Why do you not look at me?"

"I cannot look at you, Father, because lightning streams from your eyes. Your face is brighter than the sun and my eyes cannot bear it!"

"Do not be afraid, lover of God. You are now shining as brightly as I am. You are now in the fullness of the Spirit, otherwise you would not see me as I am. Come, look at me in the eyes. Look simply, without fear."[59]

I stole a glimpse, then turned away, completely overcome. I wondered then, as I do now, how fear and love differ, and which is stronger. I think love must be the stronger, no matter the brevity of its courage. In vanquishing fear, love scorches the heart, and in this manner, it bestows effortless endurance. The younger ones, both the men and the women, seek to burn always, sparkling like Chinese candles. The delicacy of love is beyond their ken. They do not prize the body's weaknesses. A red anemone blossoming at their feet would hardly draw their attention. A crippled desert oryx would not break their heart. Year by year, we older ones grow thinner and smaller. We are combustible like sticks and reeds. We salt the fire and cultivate patience in the flames. A scorched heart uproots our fears, which we offer as blazing sacrifice. We weigh the body's flaws on scales the younger ones cannot see.

My own Father has been dead forty years. I think of him each night as I watch myself in turmoil, turning on the mat. Space opens around me, it happens often, usually deep in the night, an opening broad and deep as a desert canyon. I am a mote in the eye of God. I levitate in His voluminous glory. Each breath nudges me toward a future when my dear burden, the brother before me on the mat, will himself awaken to the glorious splendor.

Notes

1. I take liberties in describing the mysteries of Eleusis—a thousand-year-old cult honored throughout the ancient world. Apart from the underground setting, the symbolic link that binds my account and historical events is the pomegranate: the fruit that Hades offers Persephone. Her eating but one seed obligates her return to the underworld for half-year intervals. For Eleusis, see Walter Burkert, *Greek Religion* (Cambridge, MA: Harvard University Press, 1985), 285–86.

2. So named because the giraffe larynx shriveled to vestigial inconsequence in the course of evolutionary history.

3. The momentum and rhythmic snap of Buddy's song "Rave On!" exploded expectations for pop music when it was released in 1958. "Rave on, it's a crazy feelin' and I know it's got me reelin.'"

4. The so-called tattoo is a Lichtenberg figure—a vascular stigmata that appears on the skin of persons struck by lightning and disappears weeks later. The figure resembles the branching pattern of a lightning bolt.

5. Superhuman sensitivity is in question. Cf. Mt. 10:29: "Are not two sparrows sold for a small coin? Yet not one of them falls to the ground without your Father's knowledge."

6. The description, most strikingly her feet, matches the Burney Relief, an ancient clay panel portraying the Mesopotamian goddess Ishtar, also known as Inanna, the Queen of the Night.

7. The beach setting, the particular sensory images, the feelings of urgency, frustration and longing recall Prufrock's plea in Eliot's "The Love Song of J. Alfred Prufrock": "I should have been a pair of ragged claws / scuttling across the floors of silent seas."

8. "I am a divine nimbus of hammered gold formed of fierce attraction," in the fifth stanza, recalls Yeats's "Sailing to Byzantium":

> Once out of nature I shall never take
> My bodily form from any natural thing,
> But such a form as Grecian goldsmiths make
> Of hammered gold and gold enameling . . . .

9. Unless otherwise noted, the quoted material in this chapter is from Valéry's *Monsieur Teste* (trans. with an intro. by Jackson Mathews [Princeton, NJ: Princeton University Press, 1989], 4, 10, 11, 12, 13, 14, 15, 17, 19, 20, 23, 26, 29, 31, 35, 39, 43, 45, 62, 63, 68, 71, 79, 80, 100, 111, 126, 132, 135–36, 138–39). Throughout the chapter, I retain Valéry's ellipses, line breaks, emphases, and indents.

10. Birth is intended as a broad metaphor. In the coming quotation, Valéry speaks of the "advent of 'Mr. Teste,'" where advent (Advent) refers obliquely to the birth of

Jesus and the first season of the ecclesiastical calendar. I view Teste as a kind of savior: personally so for Valéry, and collectively as a tutelary figure symbolizing the Cartesian spirit and Enlightenment-era ideals. For Valéry, Teste's advent signals his own reliance on rigorous, subtle, abstract intellectual enquiry in his life and work.

11. Paul Valéry, *Moi*, trans. Marthiel and Jackson Matthews (Princeton, NJ: Princeton University Press, 1975), 7.

12. The publications mentioned here include Charlotte Mandell, trans., *Monsieur Teste. Paul Valéry* (New York: NYRB Classics, 2024); Nathaniel Rudavsky-Brody, *The Idea of Perfection. The Poetry and Prose of Paul Valéry. A Bilingual Edition* (New York: Farrar, Strauss & Giroux, 2021); Paul Ryan, trans., *Collected Verse. Paul Valéry* (New York: Oxford, 2024).

13. "Teste is the Aztec priest's green obsidian blade—an elegant means of sacrifice": referring to Teste's self-discipline and ascetic spirit and his readiness to abandon the concrete in the search for transcendence. More remotely, the image refers to the ritual practices of sacrifice in ancient Mesoamerican civilizations. Such blades were used in the sacrifice of enemy captives, as the means of opening the chest and removing the still-beating heart. In the case of autosacrifice, the sacrificing person, who is typically among the nobility, emulates the gods and their creative cosmogonic power. Blood offerings were collected on paper, which was burned, the rising smoke communicating with the ancestors. The theme of sacrifice recurs later, when Teste says: "I sacrifice myself inwardly to what I would be!" For a summary of autosacrifice in Mesoamerica, see Mary Miller and Karl Taube, *An Illustrated Dictionary of the Gods and Symbols of Ancient Mexico and the Maya* (London: Thames and Hudson, 1993), 42. For blood sacrifice and its role in Aztec culture and history, see David Carrasco's *City of Sacrifice. The Aztec Empire and the Role of Violence in Civilization* (Boston: Beacon, 1999).

14. Of Heraclitus's surviving writings, see fragment 119: "A man's character is his daimon"; alternately, "Man's character is his fate." Heraclitus's belief in a principle of ceaseless flux is incompatible with Teste's insistence on perceptual clarity, incisive rational analysis, and concepts with fixed, sharp meaning. For Heraclitus, see William Harris, *Heraclitus. The Complete Fragments. Translation and Commentary and the Greek Text*, https://docplayer.net/26978323-Heraclitus-the-complete-fragments-translation-and-commentary-and-the-greek-text-william-harris-prof-emeritus-middlebury-college.html.

15. For these qualities, see Emilie Teste's letter to Paul Valéry in *Monsieur Teste*, 22–34.

16. Here and also later when Teste speaks of the *Pure Self*, he is circling the concept of the transcendental Ego, the source and organizing principle of conscious awareness. Teste's bedtime self-examination is like a case study of the phenomenologists' *epoché*, or reduction, which exposes this cognitive factor. Valéry's source in this instance is possibly Kant, although Husserl would be closer to his intent. For Valéry's remarks on Kant, see *Moi*, 78, 111, 138.

17. A quarter-century before Teste, a similar elasticity of self-identity was recognized by Rimbaud. To Izambard, in 1871, Rimbaud writes: "*Je est un autre*" ("I is someone else," according to Fowlie). Two days later, in a letter to Paul Demeny, he

sends basically the same message: "Je *est un autre*"—*I* am an other, an alien, something other, both strange and familiar to myself. The shift from *Je* to Je (the one emphasized, the other not) reflects a slightly more objective and linguistically focused perspective on the writer's part. Two days of reflection prompted this shift. The person Rimbaud is *Je*; the writer Rimbaud is Je. Rimbaud's freedom of self-invention is directed toward literary creativity, whereas Teste's is directed toward the exercise of analytical capacity. For Rimbaud's letters, see Wallace Fowlie, trans., *Rimbaud. Complete Works, Selected Letters* (Chicago: University of Chicago Press, 1966), 304.

18. The image of a navy beret suspended in a cloud of Gauloises smoke is meant to evoke a Parisian ambience and hint of mid-century French philosophy, the Existentialist account of human freedom in particular.

19. Beginning with this two-sentence paragraph, the several block quotations that conclude the examination of Teste's character and talents were written by Bradford.

20. The diminutive of wing (*l'aile*) is intended, thus my choice of winglet. *Drosophila* is a genus of fly, a fruit fly specifically.

21. The spatial characteristics of Teste's extraordinary perception resemble the third of the four formless meditations (*arūpa jhāna*s) promoted in the Buddhist Abhidhamma tradition. See D. T. Bradford, *Waves of the Glorious Splendor: Mystical Process and the Ascetic Life* (Eugene, OR: Pickwick Press, 2025).

22. The final paragraphs of *Eye of the Circle* begin here. Brackets indicate editorial additions. I have substituted asterisks for Valéry's three hand-drawn stars.

23. The repetition of *gone*, paired with the echoing /g/, recall the concluding mantra of the *Heart Sutra*: "Gaté gaté, paragaté, parasangaté, bodhi svaha." The Sanskrit—pronounced *gah-tay, gah-tay, para gah-tay, para-sun gah-tay, bodhi svaha*—is translated "gone, gone, gone beyond, gone altogether beyond. O what an awakening, all-hail!" The /g/ is hard, reminiscent of gulping, choking, and the guttural sounds of drowning. I follow Edward Conze, *Buddhist Wisdom: The Diamond Sutra and the Heart Sutra* (New York: Random House, 2001). This revered sutra conveys the doctrine of śunyata (emptiness) as taught in the Buddhist *Prajña* tradition. Valéry's exposure to such ideas was probably channeled through Schopenhauer, who mentions śunyata in *The World as Will and Representation* (vol. 1, par. 71). Referring to his early philosophical influences, Valéry remarks: "I . . . prefer Kant. But Schopenhauer will have been for me the initiator" (*Moi*, 125).

24. The insistent alliterative effect of the letter *l* merits interpretation. Did Valéry intend to infuse the sentence with the feeling of a nursery rhyme (la-lala-lala . . .), the better to sharpen his criticism of Teste? The phrase "torched your wings" alludes to Icarus's beeswax wings, which melted as he ascended toward the sun. His hubris, and his father Daedalus's, is the point of the myth.

25. See J. Hopkins, *Nicholas of Cusa's Dialectical Mysticism. Text, Translation, and Interpretive Study of De Visione Dei* (Minneapolis, MN: The Arthur J. Banning Press, 1988), 682.

26. For Valéry's opposition to religion, see *Moi* (13, 61, 347, 358). For Teste on religion, Christianity in particular, see *Monsieur Teste*, where we read that Teste stands "against the Man-God," namely Jesus Christ (141; cf. 138, 139). Valéry is particularly concerned to oppose "idols" (e.g., *Monsieur Teste*, 135–36). I should mention a

strikingly situated religious reference that concludes Teste's remarks about physical pain: "God is not far. He is what is nearest" (68). Is Holderlin nearby, his poem "Patmos" in particular, where he says the proximity of the god signals both danger and relief. *Monsieur Teste* also includes obscure sentences where Valéry says that Teste's "ideal" bears "a certain resemblance to the 'mystics'—with one vast difference, no more idols" (135).

27. For *Doppelgänger* phenomena, see D. T. Bradford, "Autoscopic Hallucinations and Disordered Self-Embodiment," *Acta Neuropsychologica* 3 (2005): 120–89.

28. All the italicized terms in this paragraph, spanning *origin* and *fulfillment*, are drawn directly from scripture. See P. Olivelle, *Upanishads* (New York: Oxford University Press, 1996), 289, 297.

29. The perfect consumer's *"shredded chest and its heartless chamber"* recalls Mesoamerican rituals of human sacrifice, as when the sternum is cut open and the heart removed from the thoracic cavity, leaving an empty (heartless) chamber. His *"trademark quetzal-feather headdress"* is like an item of royal and priestly regalia in Mayan and Aztec cultures made with feathers of the sacred quetzal. An example that possibly belonged to Moctezuma II, Cortéz's nemesis, is kept in the Museum of Ethnology in Vienna. Aztec priests celebrating the Great Feast of the Dead wore such a headdress.

30. Recalling Yeats's poem "Under Ben Bulben," which concludes with the poet's epitaph:

> Cast a cold eye
> On life, on death.
> Horseman, pass by!

Yeats's horsemen and the women accompanying them "ride the wintry dawn . . . completeness of their passions won." They could not be more different from the perfect consumer and his band of avaricious followers.

31. The creeping evergreen plants called ivy have been associated with Dionysus since the madness-inducing god first skipped from Thrace into Greece, his head and scepter coiled with ivy. See Hugh G. Evelyn-White, *Hesiod, Homeric Hymns, Homerica* [Cambridge, MA: Harvard University Press, 1998], 428–33, 450–51. Also see Euripides's *The Bacchae*, where the chorus celebrates Dionysus—"who tosses high the thyrsus, his head with ivy crowned"—and his murderous revelers. Theodor H. Gaster, *Thespis. Ritual, Myth, and Drama in the Ancient Near East* (Garden City, NY: Anchor Books, 1961), 467.

32. Recalling a crucifix in the Duoma di Ravenna. The cross itself is simply a splintered wooden post without a crosspiece, and the corpus is an armless, skeletal, bodily configuration. The garment draping the stake and corpus was in place during Easter Vigil, 2013. The congregation and the cathedral itself, for all its size and rich appointments, were as lifeless and dull as an abandoned mortuary. Only the tortured fragment emanated detectible emotion.

33. The mirrored glass paintings of geometric forms (1971–1973) are described in "Art in Due Season" (Chapter 7) and a later note.

34. The door in Duchamp's apartment was hinged along the corner of adjoining walls, between two open passageways. Entitled *Door, 11 rue Larrey*, the piece was

designed by Duchamp and constructed in 1927 by a carpenter. Other parts of this paragraph include a list of the works Duchamp called Readymades.

35. See Duchamp's assemblage *Étant donnés: 1. La chute d'eau / 2. Le gaz d'éclairage* (1946–66), housed in the Philadelphia Museum of Art. Its existence was revealed only after his death.

36. For the case in question, see D. T. Bradford, "A Therapy of Religious Imagery for Paranoid Schizophrenic Psychosis," in M. Spero, ed., *Psychotherapy of the Religious Patient* (Springfield, IL: Charles C. Thomas, 1985), 154–80.

37. An early sculpture exemplifies qualities I intended to defeat and surpass in seeking handiness, portability, simplicity—something tangible and formally beautiful, entirely remote from the clever, the ironic. The piece was a life-sized stuffed shirt, a guillotined torso that rested squarely on the table. Its decapitated and armless status was obvious from crude stitching (dotted with red paint) at the neck and sleaves of the sculpture. The breast pocket held an unsealed envelope on which the work's title—*Stuffed Shirt with Parallelepiped*—substitutes for an address. The papers inside the envelope provide a description of the piece's construction and a drawing of the cardboard sculpture hidden within the chest cavity—a parallelepiped (the second *e* is silent, the third is accented). A geometric figure of this shape is built of six parallelograms: as a square is to a cube, so a parallelogram is to a parallelepiped. I waited for viewers to tear the shirt apart, but none did. I waited to hear laughter, but no one laughed. The piece was a failure, all too clever, all too cute. I found it funny, a mock-serious verbal gesture, the concrete realization of a cliché. To whittle away at the good sense of language through concrete means was much to the point. But such whittling is light-years distance from the gasp that signals ineffability.

38. For Klee's stay in Rome, see Paul Klee. *The Diaries of Paul Klee, 1898–1918* (Berkeley: University of California Press, 1968).

39. The materials and color palette of the four glass paintings (1971–73) were limited to gold leaf, black matboard, black enamel (of different degrees of glossiness), and sheets of glass (of different thicknesses). The glass panels served as planes of display for mirrored geometric shapes made from back-silvered electroplating. The portrayed forms were limited to the rectangle and the circle. The creation of this series was meant to strangle and exhaust artistic drive in service of a higher asceticism. Their creation was treated as both a material project and a meditative exercise. Exact proportions, perfect balance, and certain contemplative states were goals. This was artistic minimalism in service of mystical ends. The alchemically tinctured thinking that informed this work was influenced by the Archetypal analysis of historical alchemy. Thus, the third painting of the series showed the mirrored segments of a square suspended within the gold outline of a circle. The circle shows obvious visual texture and is slightly elevated relative to the square. It hovers and floats and casts a shadow on the plane of the square. It might be said the circle is transcendent relative to the fixed coordinate of the square. This particular work was an aesthetic and emotional solution to the ancient problem of squaring the circle.

40. The shape of most of Mondrian's abstract paintings is either square or biased in favor of the vertical. A few are diamond-shaped, as when a square canvas is rotated at a $45°$ angle. I followed Mondrian in seeking the aesthetic effect of dynamic

equilibrium, but I also sought a more difficult format, specifically narrow horizontal canvases. As with Mondrian, only straight lines and right-angle intersections were allowed. I broadened his palette: green was permissible, as were less-than-pure primaries. Canvases were mounted on wooden boards, the better for brushwork, drawing exact outlines, and the touch I favored. I used a straightedge, unlike Mondrian, but none of his colored tape. It was while painting this series that I learned to see without the aid of verbal process. Language was made subordinate to visual and spatial perception—its inhibition freed the mind to feel and intuit in an immediate, finely calibrated, three-dimensional way. Over time, I learned to absorb (contain) all manner of spatial configurations, ranging from small objects to mountains and panoramas. Vision grades into spatial perception, which grades into imaginal incorporation. The formula can also run in the opposite direction, from inside out, whereby dark (nonvisual) shapes are felt within the body before acquiring visual form when the corresponding pattern of photons or visual memories strike the eye and the mind.

41. I combined the two perspectives. While hiking in the mountains in 1972, I made a sphere and a cube of packed snow, setting the sphere on top of the cube. Over time the geometric precision of the two shapes would come to nothing. Time would erase the artwork. The piece's construction was documented in photos and writing, and the documents framed and displayed. A topographical map was marked with the sculpture's longitude and latitude. Removing art from the sanctuary of museums was a major cultural statement of the time—a view I found exaggerated and self-defeating. Not that I didn't play along. I stenciled two-inch squares of primary colors (red, blue, yellow, also black and white) on the bumpers of cars parked or paused along Haskell Avenue, an inner-city street in Dallas, Texas. This was a down-at-the-heels variation of Mondrian's *Broadway Boogie Woogie* (1942–43). His painting exhibits flickering movement; mine churns along, spewing exhaust. Its construction was documented in a framed display. The title: *Haskell Avenue Boogie Woogie* (1974), the Haskell neighborhood being a rundown area of town. Another piece from this period toyed with biological process (decay, putrefaction, entropy) in a shadow-box assemblage made of found objects. Weathered boards of lovely Kurt Schwitters hues were used to construct an abstract landscape with pyramids set in receding perspective. A roadkill bird was suspended above the tip of the highest pyramid. The front of the box was sealed with glass. *Wired at Giza* was destroyed soon after its creation when maggots began falling from the corpse. I had not anticipated the predictable moment when Nature would intervene in this definitive manner.

42. The delicately colored painting is a photograph of John William Waterhouse's *Hylas and the Water Nymphs* (1896), its rich saturated hues as one might expect in the work of the famous Pre-Raphaelite painter.

43. These verses conclude Saying 77 of the *Gospel of Thomas* (P. Kelly, *Gospel of Thomas Commentary*, http://www.earlychristianwritings.com/thomas/index.html). Similar ideas and images are found in both Jewish and canonical Christian scripture (Is 41:4, 44:6, 48:12; Rev 22:13).

44. And its death, though real, was also temporary. A sample of later artwork will suffice—brief descriptions of several pieces completed years after the period described in "Art in Due Season": first, the collages of the Xerograph series; second, the two

keychains of the Donne series; third, a rain bonnet called *Sky Cap*; fourth, two videos of mobile handheld sculptures; and fifth, a bamboo sculpture called *Tripod*.

(1) The materials and instruments used in creating the Xerograph series include a lead pencil and reams of paper, a paper cutter and a scalpel, Scotch tape and scissors, a portable copy machine and hundreds of words and images cut from newspapers, periodicals, and personal photos. A xerograph is a collage; the entire series includes one hundred such collages. Once the series was complete, individual xerographs were photographed and printed in sepia on high quality bond, true to size (8.5" x 11"). In designing this series, I sought a cheap, easily reproducible, materially worthless medium. I intended to establish narrow aesthetic constraints, then test and exhaust them. Only black and white were allowed, Speed of execution was important—fast work that captured instantaneous flashes of coherence was favored over material polish. I meant for handwork to show, like the shine of plastic tape and the sheen of a heavy line of pencil lead. Multiple spatial perspectives could be built up in a single xerograph based on the copy machine's functions of magnification and contrast adjustment. Themes and motifs were developed over many iterations, creating series nested within the overarching series. Certain objects and places recur (e.g., the Wailing Wall, a galloping horse), as do certain characters (e.g., the artist as a luridly face-painted jester dressed in a tuxedo). Surreal strangeness infuses some xerographs, and Dada-inspired juxtapositions inform others. Direct appeals to the history of Western art are apparent (e.g., multiple sightings of The Three Graces from Botticelli's painting *Primavera*). Indigenous art and the related religious inferences are represented (e.g., the xerographic image of the vast, deeply shadowed interior of St. Paul's Cathedral, London, where Elvis Presley and the artist exchange hail-fellow greetings under the goggle eyes of the towering, feathered, long-beaked god Quetzalcoatl). The Xerograph series was developed as digital image programs were becoming popular. I rejected the false sense of creativity and technical finesse that such programs confer on their users and impose on viewers. I had no use for canned images, slick surfaces, and robotic manipulations. Combinatory action ad infinitum is not creative synthesis: the one is a sing-song mélange; the other, either stuttering or fluent, signals moments of spontaneous feeling.

(2) The materials used in creating the two works in the Donne series include laminated photos, satin ribbon, a circular silver key ring, boxing trunks, a pair of red leather boxing gloves, and two brightly colored mouthguards. In the first piece, a laminated postcard of the John Donne Memorial in St. Paul's Cathedral is attached to the keyring, which is itself attached to a shiny black mouthguard. The postcard photo shows the life-size Donne effigy sculpted by Nicholas Stone, which memorializes the great metaphysical poet and Dean of St. Paul's. This is an unusual memorial sculpture. Donne stands upright on his own funeral urn. Apart from his face, he is enveloped in a burial shroud topped with a flouncy bow or floret that anchors the shroud at the top of his

head. The shroud is stunning in the fluidity of its folds, twists, and fall. The marble seems porous, like textured glass radiating a subsurface light. Donne's eyes are shut, his head ever so slightly cocked, his expression subtly animated, as if he has found mortality (or the faking of death) an amusing turn. Reportedly, the living Donne called for a painter shortly before his death and posed as he wanted to be portrayed in effigy. In other words, Donne posed dead while alive—he posed live as if dead. The black mouthguard is impressed (literally) with the artist's upper teeth and gum. Boiled for ten seconds, then firmly bitten into—extruding all water and saliva in order to ensure a tight fit—the mouthguard is custom made. The title of this piece, which is typed on the back of the postcard, is *Batter My Heart*—the opening words of Donne's best-known Holy Sonnet: "Batter my heart, three-person'd God."

The second of the Donne pieces retains the same format but to quite different ends. In this instance, the teeth-imprinted mouthguard is fire-engine red and attached to a laminated color photo with a white satin ribbon. The photographic image, a close-up, spans the mid-thigh and solar plexus of a woman wearing gold boxing trunks with scarlet piping, her arms bent at the elbows, gloved hands raised and held in the typical defensive posture of the boxer. Sewn in full-cap letters on the red waistband of the boxing trunks is the word DONNE. The photograph of her body has been precisely outlined, cut out and affixed to highly textured flat-black paper. The effect is oddly three-dimensional—curvaceous milk-white skin and vivid satiny colors projecting forward from a black ground that sinks away into the deep space of exactly nothing. The evident artificiality of the textured ground bestows on her image and posture a claustrophobic hyper-real effect.

The two Donne pieces are nascent performance art—the mouthguards functioning as residua and negative molds of preceding bodily interventions. The second of the pieces can be read as the "prequel": the posturing and skirmishes of combative emotion preceding the surrender portrayed in the first piece. I found the second piece disturbing and sought a means of burial. The trunks were folded, name upwards, and placed in a cigar box, which I nailed shut and bound with sisal twine. A label attached to the box reads: "Donne Sealed."

(3)   Taken in hand and carefully inspected, the piece called *Sky Cap* is an 8" x 4 1/2" paper envelope with a cellophane window. Folded inside the envelope is a translucent, milky-white rain bonnet made of thin pliable plastic. The label, printed in white on a pink ground, reads: "New! / Wind & Rain / Nylon-Lined / Hair Bonnet!" Designed to protect the shellacked hair configurations favored at the time, disposable bonnets of this kind were mass-produced, as were the similar plastic raincoats called "slickers." The envelope's pastel shades resemble the colors of fairground taffy, and its message and retro lettering recall the cheery helpful-hint commercials in mid-century television and family magazines. I made significant adjustments to the contents of the envelope. Set within a pink heart on the front of the envelope is the photograph of a woman in

half-profile wearing a rain bonnet. Just above her head, visible through the cellophane window, is the midface and forehead of the Virgin Mary as portrayed in Antonello da Messina's painting *Virgin Annunciate* (1476). Antonello's Mary, which I printed in black and white on azure-blue paper, is most striking. She is attentive, visibly calm, elegant and lovely—a surprisingly modern image of unadorned beauty. From deep within her head-covering she peers through the cellophane window in a direct, unguarded, eye-to-eye manner. Now, upon opening the envelope, one finds not only the bonnet and the azure image of Mary but also a color photo of a female mannequin head, in profile, wearing a bonnet stamped with several blue five-pointed stars. The bonnet in this photo and the bonnet folded within the envelope are one and the same. *Sky Cap* resolves several pairs of opposites. This cheap dime-store sample of mass-produced material culture and sanctioned femininity grades into nested instances of mythological resonance. For example, Mary's traditional iconography includes a marine-blue cape speckled with stars. She herself is characterized as a star, the ocean depths, and the nighttime sky. The ancient Marian hymn *Ave, Maris Stella* ("Hail, Star of the Sea") says as much. To the pagan side of Mary's mythology is Zeus's impregnation of the locked-down princess Danaë through an irresistible rain of gold.

(4) *Rotating Rhinoceros* and *Shrimp Pliers* are videos of handheld sculptures in motion. The focal object of *Rotating Rhinoceros* is, indeed, a rotating rhinoceros—a gray, pliable, rubber rhinoceros that spins on the vertical axis that passes through its center of gravity, down into the chuck of the antique hand drill that functions as the rotational device. The knobs of the drill's main and side handles are made of unpainted wood; the crank is anchored in the center of a red metal drive wheel with Deco-shaped curves. Turning in full 360° circles, the rhinoceros becomes a warped blur upon attaining top speed. The speedy go-nowhere rotation and the juxtaposition of scales (the ordinarily massive rhino situated on a hand tool) reliably elicit fascination and laughter.

    Shrimp Pliers is also a kind of tool—a salmon-colored, multi-hinged plastic instrument. The two grips of its handle, which barely accommodate the user's clenched fingers, produce action at the main hinge. Toward the distal end of the pliers' lengthy jaws is a second hinge, and beyond this hinge, at the nose or tip end of the pliers, where the flat serrated gripping surfaces of normal pliers are located, are instead two rubber, highly elastic pink shrimp. The *Shrimp Pliers* video advances in a series of stop-action images: the two shrimp whip and bend in blurred curves played against a spatial field of deep black space. In an unanticipated stroke of luck, the artist's arm has been amputated at the wrist. A bodiless hand operates a useless tool in unmarked darkness.

(5) *Tripod* is one of a series of assemblages dedicated to the three-legged configuration of the tripod. A site-specific piece, it was built for display under a spotlight on the flagstone surface of an enclosed private garden. Its legs are dried, slightly curved, gradually tapering culms of giant bamboo, 15' in length

and bound together at the pivot point 12' above ground. Two objects dangle from the pivot on a transparent (and thus invisible) fishing line: a raven decoy, which hangs 5' above ground, and a bleached, horizontally positioned long bone of a large animal, which dangles 15" beneath the raven. Apart from the combination of objects, which creates a wordless sense of prophetic announcement, the power of *Tripod* depends on the positioning of its legs. The structure sags and feels depleted unless the legs are positioned in a tensely poised upright posture that conveys a stark spidery presence. The culms must form precisely determined angles below the pivot and also above, where they taper into sharp points that prick the ambient darkness. The configuration, when positioned just so, feels animated, primed to creep away under cover of darkness. Other pieces in the series include a small, desk-top tripod made of dried sticks. Suspended on a blaze-orange string from the sticks' point of intersection is a deer tooth, specifically a molar, which was painted sky blue after its extraction from a desiccated skull discovered in the mountains of southwestern Colorado.

45. Man Ray's close-up photograph of the lower glass panel of Duchamp's *Le Grande Verre* is entitled *Dust Breeding* (1920). Dust and other detritus had accumulated for a year. Man exposed the film for two hours. The resulting image appears lunar and planetary in scope and successfully creates a stupendous shift in scale.

46. The stool would serve as the base for Duchamp's sculpture *Bicycle Wheel* (1913). The cemented pieces of colored bathing caps formed *Sculpture for Traveling* (1918).

47. According to Fernand Léger, Duchamp praised the propeller to his friend Constantin Brancusi during their visit to the Paris Aviation Show in 1912. The propeller was constructed of wood rather than metal, which made all the difference. See J. Seigel, *The Private Worlds of Marcel Duchamp: Desire, Liberation, and the Self in Modern Culture* (Berkeley: University of California Press, 1997).

48. Henri-Pierre Roché's nickname for Duchamp. See Calvin Tompkins, *Duchamp: A Biography* (New York: Henry Holt, 1996).

49. Duchamp dismissive remarks refer to André Breton, founder of the Surrealist movement and author of the semi-autographical works, *Nadja* and *Amour Fou*. Breton's watchword line, "Beauty will be convulsive or will not be at all," occurs in the first of these two books.

50. The remark is consistent with Robert Motherwell's report of dining with Duchamp in the 1940s at an Italian restaurant downstairs from his studio, "where he invariably ordered a small plate of plain spaghetti with a pat of butter and grated Parmesan cheese over it, a small glass of red wine, and espresso afterward." The hagiography that would surround Duchamp had only begun to form at the time of Motherwell's visits. See Robert Motherwell, introduction to Pierre Cabanne, *Dialogues with Marcel Duchamp* (London: De Capo Press, 1971), 6.

51. Referring to *Victory Boogie-Woogie*, Mondrian's unfinished last painting.

52. Mondrian is riffing on the three-dimensional shape of the cylinder, ranging from its living human expression in Sylvia's genteel neck to its abstract variations in the paintings of Fernard Léger (1881–1955) and Umberto Boccioni (1882–1916). He

favors Léger's, which are relatively pure, versus Boccioni's, in which Futurist dynamism gravitates toward violent clashes.

53. A sleek, highly agile member of the woodpecker family.

54. Mondrian's injured angel recalls Paul Klee's print *Angelus Novus* (1920). I base Mondrian's dark portrayal of history on Walter Benjamin's interpretation of this very artwork in his "Theses on the Philosophy of History" (1942).

55. The phrase "waves of the glorious splendor" and certain other words in the first and fifth paragraphs occur in Isaac of Nineveh's Homily 52: "But as many as reflect upon the waves of the glorious splendor of the Godhead, and whose labor is on high, their minds do not turn aside with inventions and vain thoughts." Holy Transfiguration Monastery, *The Ascetical Homilies of Saint Isaac the Syrian* (Brookline, MA: Holy Transfiguration Monastery, 2011), 230.

56. Vigilance is a translation of *nipsis*, the term for a cognitive practice of meditative concentration and the screening of undesirable mental content, as advocated in the ascetic psychology of the Christian East.

57. Stillness is an English translation of *hesychia*, the term for a desirable cognitive and emotional state characterized by calm, the detached observation of mental process, and heightened receptivity to pulses of spiritual feeling, as promoted in the ascetic psychology of the Christian East.

58. The anecdote about the monk suppressing the need to urinate occurs in Isaac's twenty-first homily. Holy Transfiguration Monastery, *The Ascetical Homilies of Saint Isaac the Syrian* (Brookline, MA: Holy Transfiguration Monastery, 2011), 229–30.

59. Each man sees the other shining with light. Their respective visions occur simultaneously. My rendition of their reports of visionary luminosity is based on two sources: A. F. Dobie-Bateman, "St. Seraphim of Sarov," in G. P. Fedorov, ed., *The Way of the Pilgrim and Other Classics of Russian Spirituality* (Mineola, NY: Dover, 2003), 273–77; S. Bolshakoff, *Russian Mystics* (Kalamazoo, MI: Cistercian Publications, 1977), 135–39. For a close analysis, see D. T. Bradford, *The Spiritual Tradition in Eastern Christianity: Ascetic Psychology, Mystical Experience, and Physical Practices* (Leuven: Peeters, 2016), 73–79.

Bibliography

Bolshakoff, Serge. *Russian Mystics*. Kalamazoo, MI: Cistercian Publications, 1977.

Bradford, David T. "Autoscopic Hallucinations and Disordered Self-Embodiment." *Acta Neuropsychologica* 3 (2005) 120–89.

———. *The Spiritual Tradition in Eastern Christianity: Ascetic Psychology, Mystical Experience, and Physical Practices*. Leuven: Peeters, 2016.

———. "A Therapy of Religious Imagery for Paranoid Schizophrenic Psychosis." In *Psychotherapy of the Religious Patient*, edited by M. Spero, 154–80. Springfield, IL: Charles C. Thomas, 1985.

———. *Waves of the Glorious Splendor: Mystical Process and the Ascetic Life*. Eugene, OR: Pickwick, 2025.

Burkert, Walter. *Greek Religion*. Cambridge, MA: Harvard University Press, 1985.

Cabanne, Pierre, *Dialogues with Marcel Duchamp*. London: De Capo, 1971.

Carrasco, David. *City of Sacrifice. The Aztec Empire and the Role of Violence in Civilization*. Boston: Beacon, 1999.

Conze, Edward. *Buddhist Wisdom: The Diamond Sutra and the Heart Sutra*. New York: Random House, 2001.

Dobie-Bateman, A. F. "St. Seraphim of Sarov." In *The Way of the Pilgrim and Other Classics of Russian Spirituality*, edited by G. P. Fedorov, 273–77. Mineola, NY: Dover, 2003,

Evelyn-White, Hugh G. *Hesiod, Homeric Hymns, Homerica*. Cambridge, MA: Harvard University Press, 1998.

Fowlie, Wallace, trans. *Rimbaud. Complete Works, Selected Letters*. Chicago: University of Chicago Press, 1966.

Gaster, Theodor H. *Thespis. Ritual, Myth, and Drama in the Ancient Near East*. Garden City, NY: Anchor, 1961.

Harris, William. *Heraclitus. The Complete Fragments. Translation and Commentary and the Greek Text*. https://docplayer.net/26978323-Heraclitus-the-complete-fragments-translation-and-commentary-and-the-greek-text-william-harris-prof-emeritus-middlebury-college.html.

Holy Transfiguration Monastery. *The Ascetical Homilies of Saint Isaac the Syrian*. Brookline, MA: Holy Transfiguration Monastery, 2011.

Hopkins, Jasper. *Nicholas of Cusa's Dialectical Mysticism. Text, Translation, and Interpretive Study of De Visione Dei* (Minneapolis, MN: Arthur J. Banning, 1985).

Kirby, Peter. *Gospel of Thomas Commentary*. http://www.earlychristianwritings.com/thomas/index.html.

Klee, Paul. *The Diaries of Paul Klee, 1898-1918*. Berkeley: University of California Press, 1968.

Mandell, Charlotte, trans. *Monsieur Teste. Paul Valéry.* New York: NYRB Classics, 2024.

Miller, Mary, and Karl Taube. *An Illustrated Dictionary of the Gods and Symbols of Ancient Mexico and the Maya.* London: Thames and Hudson, 1993.

Rudavsky-Brody, Nathaniel. *The Idea of Perfection. The Poetry and Prose of Paul Valéry. A Bilingual Edition.* New York: Farrar, Strauss & Giroux, 2021.

Ryan, Paul, trans. *Collected Verse. Paul Valéry.* New York: Oxford, 2024.

Seigel, Jerrold. *The Private Worlds of Marcel Duchamp, Desire, Liberation, and the Self in Modern Culture.* Berkeley: University of California Press, 1997.

Valéry, Paul. *Moi,* translated with an intro. by Jackson Mathews. Princeton, NJ: Princeton University Press, 1975.

———. *Monsieur Teste,* translated with an intro. by Jackson Mathews. Princeton, NJ: Princeton University Press, 1989.